Frat Hell

Violent Circle: Book Two

S.M. Shade

Cover art by Ally Hastings at Starcrossed Covers.
Interior formatting by Angela at That Formatting Lady

Dedication

This book is dedicated to my son, who insisted I never dedicate a romance book to him because it's creepy. Well, who the hell does he think he is? He can't tell me what to do, so...

To Nate,
Love Mom

Where to find S.M. Shade

I have a private book group where no one outside of the group can see what you post or comment on. It's adults only and is a friendly place to discuss your favorite books and authors. Drama free. I also host an occasional giveaway, and group members get an early peek at covers, teasers, and exclusive excerpts.

You can join here:
https://www.facebook.com/groups/694215440670693

You can also follow or friend me on Facebook:
https://www.facebook.com/authorsmshade

Or like my page:
https://www.facebook.com/smshadebooks

Chapter One

Noble

I swear this place always smells like a bar threw up in a locker room. It's one of the few reasons I'll be happy to move back home next year. One of the neighbors dubbed our place Frat Hell a few years ago and it isn't far off. Probably why the name stuck.

Denton pokes his head into my room. "Dude? Are you playing with your meat today?"

"At eleven," I mumble, rolling over and pulling a pillow over my head. "What time is it?"

"Nine. The chick Kenny was banging last night didn't leave quietly."

"They never do." Kenny is the biggest man whore I've seen. He brings home a different woman three nights a week and isn't all that respectful when he asks them to leave. Being awakened by a cursing, pissed off woman isn't out of the ordinary.

"I dragged Trey and Kenny out of bed to clean house. It's their turn. Do you want to grab some donuts before work?"

A loud bang shakes the apartment, followed by laughter from Kenny and Trey. Decision made. "Absolutely. Give me five minutes."

Denton nods and leaves me to get dressed.

Ugh, another day arguing with customers over pork chops and ground beef. I've been working at the meat department of the local supercenter for over three years. Yeah, insert witty pun about handling my meat here. I swear I've heard them all.

It's not a bad job on some days. It could be worse. Trey works fast food and from the stories he tells, I'm happy to stay right where I am, at least until school ends. This was supposed to be my last year, but I've been offered a scholarship which will pay for me to pursue a master's degree. It means two more years of school, but I've decided to do it.

Knowing I have a future ahead of me that doesn't include mopping up blood and tossing out rotted meat keeps me from partying as hard as the other guys, especially now, when I have to keep my GPA up to hang onto the scholarship.

Trey and Kenny have managed to make it from their beds to the couch and recliner in the living room. "Don't you assholes have to work?" I gripe.

"Tonight," Trey replies. "Kenny got fired."

"Again?" I laugh. "What did you do this time?" Since I've known him, Kenny has worked at a burger joint, the supercenter, and a car wash. His current job is—or was—as a clerk for the local drugstore.

Kenny raises his shoulders. "Not a damn thing!"

"You asked a woman who was buying condoms if they were *for here or to go*," Trey snorts.

"They have no sense of humor," Kenny grumbles, grabbing the bong.

"Seriously?" I slip on my jacket. "Already?"

Kenny grins up at me. "Yes, dad. This is what's known as a wake and bake. Try really hard to think back about three years and I'm sure the concept is still in there somewhere."

I grab the bong out of his hands and hand it to Trey. "Says the guy whose daddy pays for everything. Later, assholes."

Denton appears and follows me out the door, tossing back an order. "Those dishes better be fucking spotless!"

We're headed toward my car when Neal, my neighbor from a few doors down, approaches with a red headed woman I've never seen before. If this is his girlfriend, he's definitely chosen well.

"Neal, how's it going?" I pause on the sidewalk as they walk up to me.

"Can't complain. Glad the damned rain finally stopped."

It's rained more in the last few days than it has for months. Neal works at the full-service car wash across town so rainy days means they close up and he doesn't get paid.

Smiling at the woman beside him, he continues, "I just wanted to introduce Veronica. She and her son, Aiden, just moved in to Cassidy's old place."

Ah, fresh meat. The guys will be all over this poor girl. I reach and shake her hand. "I'm Noble. Welcome to Violent Circle. Be ready for anything."

Her face lights up as she laughs. "Yeah, that's what I've heard. It's nice to meet you."

Denton joins us and doesn't bother to hide the way his gaze travels up and down her body. At least he doesn't throw out any skeevy pickup lines. "I'm Denton." He gestures toward our apartment. "We live right there if you ever need anything."

Her eyes widen. "Oh, you live together?"

I can't help myself. And from the look on Denton's face, he knows what's coming. I wrap my arm around his waist and tilt my head to rest on his shoulder. "For over three years now."

Denton jerks away. "Don't listen to him. He's always—"

I lay a finger across his lips. "Babe, shush, it's okay. We're in a safe place. Veronica isn't going to judge you." My gaze shifts to her as I say her name.

"Of course not!" she replies brightly. "I think that's fantastic. We'll have to get together for dinner sometime. I don't really know anyone here."

The struggle taking place on Denton's face is priceless. Does he keep arguing and make it look like he's in the closet, or take the opportunity to hang out with her again and then tell her the truth? Eventually, he chooses to stay quiet.

Neal is having a hard time keeping a straight face, but she doesn't seem to notice.

"That sounds great. We look forward to it. It was nice meeting you, but we have to get going. Going to hit the gym before work." I grin in Denton's direction. "Not all of us are lucky enough to have naturally slim thighs." Gesturing to my car, I call, "Door is unlocked, babe."

Veronica smiles, and she and Neal walk away while I climb into my car where my shoulder is met with Denton's fist.

"Asshole! She was hot!"

"Yeah, she was." I put the car in gear and start toward Foster's Bakery.

"Just because Jani keeps blowing you off doesn't mean you have to cock block the rest of us," he grumbles.

"She's not avoiding me!"

She is. For over a month now, ever since she dared me, and I accepted. Never underestimate what a guy is willing to do to get the girl he wants. In my case, I walked a makeshift runway in bondage gear. It was cold. I don't recommend it.

"She lives four apartments away and you never see her," he points out.

"It just so happens, I'm going to her place after work today. And don't be a sulky bitch. I'm sure Neal has already told Veronica the truth. You'd better work fast, though, before Kenny finds out there's fresh meat in the neighborhood."

"Nah, he won't fuck the ones who live too close, remember?"

"That's true."

We both order a couple of donuts and a coffee before taking a seat at a corner table. "We need to put a foot in Kenny's ass," Denton says. "He's flunking out of college."

Sipping my lava disguised as coffee, I nod. "I heard. I've tried to talk to him. Everyone parties through college, but he's taking it too far. He barely scraped through freshman year. I told him he has to find a balance, make sure his grades are a priority."

"Do you think you got through his thick ass skull?"

Sighing, I shake my head. "I doubt it. All I managed to do was earn the nickname 'Dad'."

Denton scoffs. "That's half the problem. His parents pay

for everything. He's never had to worry about where his next meal is coming from. If the day comes when he's on his own, he'll be screwed. He'll never find a job. He's burned every bridge in town."

Kenny is a good guy. He's always quick to help someone when they need it, but he doesn't seem to give one shit about his future. "His parents are coming to visit next week. Maybe they can straighten him out." I scarf down my second donut and wipe the crumbs from my mouth. "What happened with you and that chick you were seeing? You going to introduce her to the guys?"

Denton shakes his head and groans. "Uh...no. That's over. You know, I never put much stock in the whole blondes are stupid stereotype, but that girl was living proof."

"Fuck off," I snort, running my hand through my blond hair.

Amusement seeps into his voice as he explains. "I'm serious. The girl called nine-one-one to ask if a tablespoon is the big spoon or the little one. A cop showed up at the door to lecture her on the improper use of an emergency line. I never get embarrassed, but that shit was embarrassing."

Laughing, we toss our trash and head out the door. "Dodged a bullet there, it sounds like."

"Damn right."

When we return to the apartment, it's full of pot smoke, but Trey and Kenny are busy cleaning the kitchen. I grab my name badge and head off to work.

Kori, my manager and the biggest bitch I've ever met in my life, glares at me as I enter the break room. "The truck didn't get put away last night," she snaps. "The cooler is full of pallets."

"Good morning to you, too," I reply cheerfully, grabbing a cup of coffee from the machine.

I've learned this is the best way to get under her skin. It kills her that she can't make me mad or upset like she can the other employees doomed to work under her. She hates me for some reason, and I know she'd love to get me fired. Fortunately, that isn't in her power, and Niall, the manager who works above her, likes me. In fact, we play video games together online on our nights off.

Fuming, she continues to glare at me when I take a seat across the room beside one of the cashiers. "That truck is going to put us behind!"

"I'm not on the clock for another twenty minutes."

One of the general managers, Jimmy, walks in and greets me with a smile. "Noble, how are you doing?"

"Can't complain. I just won a scholarship to pay for two more years at college. So, it appears I won't be putting in my notice before graduation after all." Smiling, I take a sip of coffee and glance at Kori. "Looks like you're stuck with me."

"Glad to hear it." Jimmy sits across from me with his lunch. The shifts here are so crazy, there are employees eating lunch or hanging out in the break room at all hours.

Jimmy turns to Kori. "The fresh wall is wiped out. Didn't you get a truck last night?"

"Yes, but apparently Noble didn't bother to put it away."

Chuckling, I shrug. "It might be because I had yesterday off."

If Kori's lips press together any harder, she'll swallow herself. Jimmy's next remark doesn't help. "I know your closer called in, but you came in at five this morning, didn't you?"

Kori, stoop so low as to actually work instead of barking orders and complaining? Never.

"Well, I'm on at eleven, so I'd better get moving," I announce, turning to Jimmy. "I'll start with the fresh wall."

"If you ever want to make the jump over to the pharmacy, I need someone to replace Charlene," he offers.

Kori's face is getting redder by the second.

"I appreciate the offer, but I'm good where I am."

Nothing can wipe the smile from my face as I leave the room, listening to Kori try to excuse her laziness. I can't wait to tell the others. Three other employees work with me in the meat department, and none of us can stand Kori. She's the definition of an awful manager. It's no secret she fucks up every department she runs. She was front line manager, but it was a catastrophe. They promoted her to section manager and stuck her in the meat department to get rid of her, which pretty much tells you how screwed up this place is.

Unlike my coworkers, I don't let it get to me. This is all temporary. I'm headed for better things, and a miserable bitch who's facing a lifetime of this place isn't going to ruin my day. Humming, I clock in, throw on my white coat that always makes me want to play doctor, and get to work restocking the wall of fresh meat.

Another day. Another dollar.

Jani's mother, Aubrey, answers the door when I knock, and lets me in with a wide smile. "Noble, Jani's in the shower. Have a seat."

A reality show blares from the television as I sit on the couch across from Aubrey. "Do you two have a date?"

"Yep. She just doesn't know it yet."

Aubrey chuckles as the bathroom door pops open. "This should be interesting."

Jani walks into the room, wearing nothing but a towel, with another wrapped around her head in that magic way women seem to know. It looks like she walks into an invisible wall when she sees me, and her towel slips a bit at her abrupt stop.

Aubrey steps out of the room as Jani demands, "What the hell are you doing here?"

"We have a date."

Huffing, she shakes her head. "No, we don't."

"Think back really hard, and try to remember a magical day in October when I wore leather gear and a ball gag just for you."

Despite her attitude, she bites back a smile. "It was quite a sight."

Yeah, to the whole town. When the adult store Jani works at was throwing a fundraiser to keep them from getting tossed out of town, Jani dared me to join the lingerie show wearing bondage gear. I did it, and now she owes me a date.

My gaze sweeps over her, and I'm glad I wore loose jeans. "So are you. Now, about that date. I have no objection to us spending it naked, but I do have another idea."

"Does it include finding another woman to harass endlessly?"

Laying my palm on my heart, I get to my feet. "Harass?"

"Yes, you know…badger, annoy, pester."

Sighing, I cross my arms. "I did not come here to be insulted by a giant Q-tip. Now, Cassidy told me you have the weekend off, so I'll pick you up at ten tomorrow morning. Dress warm, it's going to be cold where I'm taking you."

"You're never going to give up, are you?"

"One date. If you still don't like me, I promise I'll never bother you again."

Jani unfurls the towel on her head, letting her dark hair fall to her shoulders. "I like you, Noble. You just aren't my type."

"What?" I look her in the eye. "Sorry, everything went all slow motion for a moment."

Rolling her eyes, she starts drying her hair with the towel. "I'm not going to sleep with you. You really should move on to another victim."

"Trust me, it'll be way too chilly for me to even think about releasing the dart of love. Just a nice, normal date."

"Fine. I'll be ready."

The fact she agreed is still sinking in when Aubrey walks back into the room. "You heard her, Aubrey. I have a witness. I'm picking her up in the morning."

Aubrey laughs and grabs the remote control. "I'll swear to it under oath. She needs a little action to rattle her out of that mood."

Jani runs her palm over her face. "Aren't you missing a Kardashian show or something?"

"I don't watch the Kardashians! But Dance Moms is just coming on if you want to watch. Did you know the teacher is going to prison? I swear, this show is crazy."

"Ten o'clock," I repeat, as I head for the door. "Later,

beautiful."

It's only a little past six when I get home, but our resident drunk is already trashed. It's nothing out of the ordinary. This is Violet Circle, nothing much is surprising here. As you probably already figured out, my apartment complex is built in a circle. Someone has added an N to our street sign, making it Violent Circle, which is occasionally true, but most of the time, we just get free entertainment from the neighbors. Like today.

Barney lives on the other end of the long loop, so I don't see him much. He doesn't generally stagger down this far, but he's in prime form today. He's earned the nickname Barney, like the guy from The Simpsons, and answers to it more than he does Barry, his actual name.

"Barney! How's it going?" Trey calls out. He and the rest of the guys are hanging out on the front step.

"Need two dollars!" he slurs. "You got two dollars?" He barely gets the words out before he stumbles over air and falls down hard on his ass.

Laughing, Trey and Denton get up to go help him. I catch up to them as they get him to his feet. "Knobble, you gots two dollarsh?" he slurs, and Trey snorts out a laugh.

"Knobble, that one's going to stick."

"Shut up and get behind him before he busts his ass again."

We all start walking him back toward his apartment. We've almost made it when one of the neighborhood cops pulls up. Barney is well known by them, and hasn't had a license or a car in years because of his drinking. They usually leave him be if he isn't causing any trouble, but wandering around like this, he's begging for another public intox charge.

"Officer Green, how's it going?" Denton asks.

"Not too bad." Officer Green turns his attention to Barney. "Barry, you okay? You look a little unstable."

"He's fine," Trey says before Barney can try to speak and show just how trashed he is. It's bad enough he's leaning against me. "He's just been up all night. Needs some sleep. We'll get him back to his apartment."

Officer Green laughs and shakes his head. "All right boys,

get him home." He points a finger at Barney. "Get inside and stay there, Barry. If I see you out again tonight in this condition, you'll be spending the night in jail."

Barney gives him a gap-toothed smile. "Sure. Hey. You gots two dollarsh?"

"For fuck's sake," I murmur.

Officer Green laughs and drives away. We're only a few feet from Barney's place when he makes an abrupt stop.

"Come on, man, just a few more steps," I tell him.

He looks down at his darkening crotch. "Hey, someone pissed m'pants."

Denton looks at me, and we both crack up. "We'll try to catch the guy, Barney," Denton assures him.

Laughing, Trey grabs at Barney as he tips too far back., "Let's just get him home. I got shit to do."

"Let's hope he doesn't," Denton quips.

We finally manage to deposit him on his couch and leave him to sleep it off. It won't be the first time—or probably the tenth—that he'll wake up in piss. It's sad, but there's nothing we can do. Multiple people have tried to get him into a rehab, and everyone in the circle even agreed to pitch in some money to cover what his insurance doesn't, but he won't go. You can't help someone who doesn't want it.

"It's your turn to make dinner," Trey says to me when we get home.

"Well aware, ginger tits."

Trey lifts up his shirt and shakes his moobs at me. "I think I've gone down a cup size, so don't skimp on the cheese, Knobble." Trey may be a big guy, but he owns it. And it doesn't seem to hurt him when it comes to women.

After dinner, I get all the supplies together I'll need for my date with Jani tomorrow. I know she thinks I'm just trying to get her into bed, and while I certainly wouldn't say no if she offered, I really do like hanging out with her.

I want to do something unique. Something she'll remember.

Chapter Two

January

I've put off this date as long as I could. I really thought Noble would give up and move on to someone else, but I greatly underestimated his stubbornness. What I said to him was true. I do like him, but I'm tired of dating these immature guys who have no plans for their future. My job at Scarlet Toys may not be glamorous, but I have my mother to take care of, and it pays the bills. Eventually, I plan to go back to school and study business management, maybe open a store of my own. I need someone who isn't focused on smoking weed and partying all the time.

All Noble told me about our date was to dress warm, so I throw on two layers of clothing. I leave my hair down to keep my neck warm and grab a knit cap in case it's really chilly. There's no predicting the weather here anymore. It's the last week of November, but the highs are still in the sixties. Last year at this time, we had snow.

"Jani! There's a handsome young man in here looking for you!" Mom calls.

"Tell him to get lost. I have a date with an annoying, average looking neighbor!" A quick glance in the mirror, and I'm ready as I'll ever be.

"Average looking!" he scoffs when I step into the living

room. "I'll have you know my mom and her friends told me I could be a model!"

He's joking, but, honestly, he probably could. Standing there in my living room, dressed in jeans and a hoodie, he looks like he could've stepped off of a billboard. Messy blond hair falls over his forehead, and his light blue eyes twinkle with mischief. A dimple pops out when he grins at me.

"See, you're checking me out right now."

Damn it. I was.

"Shut up...I was thinking. Should I wear sneakers or boots?"

"Whatever you aren't afraid to get dirty," he replies.

Oh no. Where is he taking me?

After saying goodbye to my mother, we're on our way. "Are you going to tell me where we're heading now?"

Noble grins and turns onto the highway. "The east fork of White River."

My summers were spent at camp when I was a kid, so I'm no stranger to the outdoors, but Noble doesn't strike me as the type. "Are we fishing?"

"Yep. But not for fish. Have you ever heard of magnet fishing?"

Fishing for magnets? "Uh...no."

"You tie a strong magnet to a rope and drag it through the water. It'll pick up anything metal. We'll catch a lot of junk, but that's half the fun, sorting through to find the good stuff."

That actually does sound like fun. "Kind of like metal detecting. I had a metal detector when I was young, but I never found much except bottle caps and bits of wire."

"With magnet fishing, it's a lot of fish hooks. I've found a few phones, but none that would ever power on."

We spend the rest of the thirty-minute drive talking about music and our favorite bands. We have a lot of them in common. Noble is different when he isn't around his friends. Instead of joking all the time and replying with smart assed answers, he's more subdued and talkative. I know I'm guilty of the same thing.

Noble has definitely been here before because he knows

right where to go to park, and where to find an easy path down to the riverbank. He slings a large backpack onto his back and grabs my hand before we start down the path. Hmm…frat boy likes to hold hands…didn't see that coming. It's sweet.

The wind coming off of the river is freezing, and I pull my knit cap down over my ears. No wonder he said to dress warm. He unloads the bag, and lays out two thick magnets wrapped in cloth, a length of rope, two plastic bottles, and two pair of gloves. He proceeds to cut the top off of the plastic bottles. He slides each of them onto the rope before attaching a magnet to the end.

"So, we just chuck it out there and drag it in?" I ask.

"Pretty much. Once you get the hang of it, you'll be able to feel if you've caught something or if it's just trapped between rocks. It's not very rocky here, so it's a good beginner spot."

A cute smile flashes across his face as he asks me, "Are you ready?"

"Let's do it."

"Later, beautiful, for now, we fish."

A giggle escapes me as I reach for a rope. "Just show me how far to throw it."

"We'll do the first one together. Then we have to put some space between us so our magnets don't find each other. When they get stuck together, they're a bitch to pull apart."

Handing me a pair of gloves, he grabs the rope, and we walk to the edge of the water. He throws the magnet hard, and it splashes as it disappears underwater. The current pulls a little on the rope, but the magnet is heavy enough to sink.

Standing beside me, he says, "Just pull it nice and slow."

"Are we still talking about the rope?" Before he can reply, I feel a slight tug. "I think I have something!"

Noble puts a hand on the rope in front of mine and tugs a little. "It's something big."

Excitement floods through me as I imagine all the things that could have ended up in the river. What if it's a safe? A safe full of money!

"Keep pulling, steady and slow so you don't lose it."

The object is getting closer and closer, a little more and I'll be able to see it. When I pull again, the rope won't budge. "It's stuck on something."

I try to hand Noble the rope, but he moves behind me instead and reaches around my sides, gripping the rope along with me. Together, we manage to get it moving again without losing the mystery object.

My squeal of excitement makes Noble laugh. "You aren't having fun on our date, are you?" he teases.

"As long as you understand I'm keeping all the money we find in the safe we're dragging up." His laughter scares away some nearby birds. "It's like finding buried treasure," I add.

"Don't worry, there's only one booty I'm interested in."

"Pirate puns, really?"

"So, I'll be swabbing my own deck?"

Laughing together, we give the rope one last heave and the object clangs, flips over, and lands in the mud.

"Don't spend all that money in one place," Noble snorts.

"A shopping cart? Who throws a shopping cart in the river?"

Noble sloshes through the mud and yanks the magnet free. "It's not the first one I've snagged."

"What's the best thing you've caught?"

He turns and grins at me, giving me the urge to kiss that little dimple. "Your eye."

It was a completely lame response. So why do I want to throw him down in the mud and ravage him? My lack of reply just makes his smile broaden.

"Ha! No comeback *and* you're blushing. I think I won that one."

"And what do you think you've won?"

Noble throws the magnet back out. "Well, another date, at least."

"We aren't even finished with this one." I take the rope from him.

"No, all our dates have to end with a kiss."

The thought of his lips on mine sends a spike of excitement through me, but I can't let him see it.

Keeping my voice as nonchalant as possible, I ask, "So, if I kiss you now, we can call it a day?"

Sauntering up to me, his grin falls, and his voice deepens. "Do you want me to kiss you, January?"

The rope in my hand is forgotten, dropped to the bank as his hands cup my jaws. His palms are warm against my face. He presses his soft lips to mine for a moment, then retreats, before kissing me again, just as tenderly. It's the sweetest kiss I've ever been given, and my stomach explodes in butterflies like a teenage girl. It feels wonderful.

I'm so screwed.

Without a word, he picks up the rope and hands it to me again. Silence reigns until I pull the magnet back in. This time there's a ring, a shotgun shell, two fish hooks, and a spoon.

Noble wipes the mud off the ring with his glove and we can see an inscription inside. *To my dear Maeetta, the loveliest woman.*

"It's a wedding ring. I wonder how long it's been down there?" I remark.

Noble holds it up where the light is better. "Hard to tell. It's not in bad shape."

"Maybe I can find the owner and return it!" I exclaim, excited at the prospect.

"With a name like Maeetta, she can't be too hard to find," Noble agrees. "Want to go again?"

"Yes!"

My enthusiasm makes him smile. We spend the next two hours throwing the ropes and dragging them back, often coming up empty. By the time a soft rain begins to fall, we have a small pile of odds and ends. Watches, phones, coins, fish hooks, bolts, and some chunks of metal that are unrecognizable. Nothing else as big as the shopping cart.

"One more time," I insist, and we both throw out our ropes. Mine comes back empty, but when Noble holds his up, a metal bracelet dangles from the magnet.

"Too bad," I remark, checking it out. "It's pretty. I have a thing for stars. But it's damaged."

Noble sticks it in his bag along with some of the other bits of metal.

"What do you do with all that junk?"

"I don't want to just leave it to pollute the river. Whatever small things I pull out, I just chuck in a box, and drop the box at the recycling center when it's full."

Noble furls up the ropes and puts everything away in the backpack before slinging it on his back. He grabs my hand and we start making our way back up the path. It's less of a path and more of a mudslide now that the rain has started.

Laughing, we slip and slide until get about halfway up. My foot slides, but I manage to catch it on a root, and brace my hand against a tree. Noble isn't so lucky. The soft earth gives way beneath his feet, and a small yelp leaps from his mouth before he goes tumbling back down the slope.

Tumbling isn't the right word. The three backward somersaults he manages on the way down would be impressive if he were trying to do them. He finally stops himself, and lies back in the mud. Trying my best not to laugh—damn what I would give to have that on video—I rush back down to check on him.

"Noble? Are you okay?" Shit. What if he broke his neck and I'm standing here laughing at him?

Staring up at me with a straight face, he says, "I think I saw my own ass crack."

"I don't think that's physically possible," I laugh, kneeling beside him.

"Neither did I. But I swear I mooned myself."

"Are you hurt?"

"Nope, just waiting on the judge's score. You saw that shit, right?" His cheeks redden, and I realize he's embarrassed. Ugh, why does he have to be so adorable?

"It was a solid eight."

"Only eight?" He starts to sit up, but I push him back and stop his next words with my lips. This kiss isn't as soft and gentle as the last one. His hand grips the back of my head, and he moans as I slip my tongue between his lips. The cold mud seeping through our clothes and the icy rain falling on us is no match for the heat that washes over me when he brushes my tongue with his.

"Are you trying to kiss it better?" he asks when we break apart.

"Did it help?"

I grab his hand, and he gets to his feet. "Absolutely. I'll do a swan dive into the mud if that's my reward."

The wind picks up, and I start to shiver. "Come on," he says. "Let's get to the car where it's warm."

"We're going to get your car all wet and muddy."

"It's fine. Neal works at the car wash. I'll take it to him tomorrow."

It takes a few minutes, but we manage to make our way back up the path. Noble opens the trunk and pulls out a blanket, wrapping it around my shoulders. He hands me the keys. "I have some spare clothes in here. You want to start the car and get it warm?"

After I'm buckled in the passenger seat, enjoying the warm air that blows from the vents, I turn to see him pull a shirt over his head. His body is lean and muscled, with a smattering of dark hair. I'm disappointed that I only get a glance before his shirt covers it.

I can't help but chuckle when he gets in wearing a pair of board shorts with fish printed on them and a thin white tee.

"What? You don't like my manly fishy shorts?"

"Very sexy." I point one of the vents at him. He has to be freezing.

"Lucky I forgot to take my stuff out of the trunk last time I went swimming."

The drive home is relaxing, with music playing and the steady beat of rain on the windows. When we get close to home, he reaches over and interlaces his fingers with mine. It's sweet.

"You don't have to get out," I tell him when he pulls up in front of my apartment. "It's freezing." Looking up, I sigh. "And my mom is haunting the door, pretending not to watch us."

"Then I'll have to pretend to be a gentleman." He leans over and plants a soft, quick kiss on my lips. "Now, admit you had fun."

"Fine, I had fun."

He grins. "So you'll go out with me again?"

"It's hard to resist a guy limber enough to see his own ass."

"We're a brave few," he replies, with a wise nod.

"I'll see you later." The cold air strikes me as I get out of the car.

He waves at my mom as he drives off, and she quickly moves away from the door.

Cassidy steps out onto her porch, waving to me as I park in her driveway. Now that she's moved from Violent Circle, we don't hang out as much as we used to, but I still see her at work.

"Some new chick moved into your old apartment," I tell her, once we're inside. I'm lounging on her couch while she sits across from me in a recliner. "Her name's Veronica. I want to hate her."

"What's wrong with her?"

"She isn't you."

Cassidy laughs and throws a pillow at me. "I only moved fifteen minutes away."

"If I can't stumble home from your place drunk at four a.m. it's too far."

Wyatt, her fiancé, walks in. "I'm happy to drive your drunk ass home whenever you need, Jani." He glances at the clock. "I thought you had the early shift at Scarlet Toys." Wyatt is the owner of a sex toy shop that opened in town last year. It's where Cassidy met and fell in love with him. It's a nice place to work.

"I switched with Martha. Cass, tell your man to stop micromanaging."

Wyatt picks up the pillow from Cass's lap and drops it on my head.

"Okay, spill it. You went out with Noble yesterday. I want details."

Wyatt wanders out of the room at the first sign of our girl

talk. "It was fun. Have you ever heard of magnet fishing?"

"Yeah, it's where they throw magnets in lakes and stuff to see what they can pick up, right?"

"Pretty much. He took me to the river to try it."

Cassidy eyes me. "And?"

"And it was fun."

She pulls her legs up, tucking them beneath her. "Cut the shit, Jani. There's something you aren't telling me."

"I might have kissed him."

A smile bursts across her face. "You kissed him?"

"Only after he kissed me!"

"So, are you going out again?"

"Yeah, next weekend. He showed me his hobby, so I'm going to show him mine."

Her face turns serious. "I hope you really give him a chance."

"Why wouldn't I?"

Cass rolls her eyes. "You always find something wrong with the guys you date. Like Charlie. He was so nice."

"The boy ate cheese puffs with a spoon."

A snort of laughter comes from the doorway, and Wyatt enters. He grabs Cass up like she's weightless, sits in the recliner and plants her on his lap. She goes on like nothing happened. "Or that guy you met last year at the water park."

"He sucked in bed! His cock looked like a sad manatee, and he rubbed my clit like he was trying to get bird shit off his car window."

Cass laughs, curling up against Wyatt. "Well, the date was fun. How was the kiss?"

"Amazing," I confess. "Like I said, we're going out again Friday. I'm going to take him to the old asylum."

"Sounds romantic," Wyatt scoffs.

"Says the man who proposed to his girl using sex toys."

It may sound strange, but I love exploring old buildings. It's risky since I don't always have permission and I'm technically trespassing. Plus, homeless people and junkies sometimes take up residence there, but I never go alone. The asylum is a spooky place, but we'll be going in the daylight, and Noble may as well know my weirdness from the beginning.

"We need a girl's night Saturday then. We both get off work at eight. We can come back here."

"Sounds good to me." I get to my feet. "I should get to work. The owner is a real hard ass."

Cass laughs and reaches under Wyatt. "Nah, it's a little squishy."

Chapter Three

Noble

It's been a long day of classes, then work, and all I want to do when I get home is shower and crash. Tomorrow will be dedicated to studying, but Friday I have another date with Jani. At the ungodly hour of 6 a.m. She's getting her revenge for me not telling her where I was taking her last week. I don't have a clue where we're going.

I'm shocked at the state of the apartment when I walk in. It's spotless, without a whiff of pot smoke in the air. Trey is scarfing down a bowl of cereal at the kitchen table, and Kenny is wiping down the counter.

"Damn it! Stop dripping milk on the floor! I just mopped!" Kenny exclaims.

The doorjamb creaks as I lean against it. "Am I having a stroke?"

Trey gestures toward Kenny with a spoonful of milk in his hand and slops some on the table. "His parents are coming tomorrow. For some reason, he thinks a clean apartment will help them overlook the fact they're paying tuition for him to party and fuck his way through campus."

Kenny glares at him and wipes up the milk. "None of that talk while they're here."

Denton walks in, and he's apparently been listening. "Good luck with that. Your dad called me. They're coming to stage an intervention."

Kenny's head whips around to face him. "I'm not an alcoholic!"

"It's not about the alcohol. It's about going to class and taking care of your responsibilities."

Kenny scoffs and leans back against the counter, crossing his arms. "Like you guys don't get trashed and fuck chicks all the time?"

Denton pulls a can of cola out of the fridge. "Sure I do, but I also go to my classes, do my coursework, and work at the financial aid office. Moderation, buddy. That's what it's about."

"Everyone parties too much freshman year, but you have to get serious eventually. Unless you want to work some shit job forever," Trey adds.

Kenny shakes his head. "You guys, maybe, but I have money."

Denton speaks up. "No, your parents have money. Big difference."

"What would you do if they cut you off tomorrow?" Trey asks. "You'd be screwed."

Denton and Trey continue to try to talk some sense into Kenny while I head off to shower and get ready for bed.

I'm just about to doze off when my phone beeps with a message from Jani.

Jani: Mom is watching a reality show about naked people in a forest. FML.

Me: Are there at least women with nice boobs?

Jani: No, these are not people anyone would want to see naked.

Me: You could come here and see me naked.

Jani: Pass

Noble: So, just a dick pic, then?

Jani: Can you zoom in close enough to fit the little feller in the shot?

Noble: I can have Denton take it from across the room. It might all fit in the frame.
Jani: Going to sleep now.
Noble: Me too, beautiful. Good night.
Jani: Good night. See you Friday.

I have no desire to hang around for Kenny's intervention, so as soon as I wake, I shower, grab my stuff, and head to the library. I should have gone to the public library instead of the college library. I'm barely settled into a corner table when I feel eyes on me.

Two girls sit across from each other, making no effort to hide the fact they're staring at me. My first couple of years here, I may have whored it up a bit too much. In my defense, I was fresh out of high school, and surrounded by girls who followed me around like I might have the secret to immortal youth. I'm not trying to be conceited. I don't think I'm any more attractive than the next guy.

No, the frenzy started because of a comment a girl made in my freshman year. We slept together a couple of times—if you count banging in her dorm room sleeping together—and she promptly spread the word amongst her friends. From that moment on I had a new nickname whether I liked it or not.

Porn Penis.

Yeah, she told her friends I had a dick that belonged in a porno, and voila, I'm drowning in offers. I admit I totally went with it at first, what nineteen-year-old guy wouldn't? Believe it or not, fucking a different girl every week got old...and lonely. It appears I've screwed myself though, because my reputation precedes me as the guy with a big cock who loves to share it. It's all the girls here want from me.

I'm glad Jani doesn't go to school. She has no idea about the nickname or how I got it. Now that I'm ready to settle down, I'm afraid my past is going to bite me on the ass. And not in the way I like.

The two girls keep looking my way, smiling and giggling, flirting to the best of their abilities, considering we're in a silent library. I usually try to ignore them when this happens, but I go a different route this time.

Do you know you can creep people out by doing normal stuff at an extra slow pace? It's funny as hell. Slowly, I look up from my book and stare at one of the giggling girls. A fraction at a time, I let a smile inch across my face, until it's wide and makes me look insane. I keep staring at her with the psycho look until her grin falters. They both watch as I reverse and ever so slowly bring my face back to an impassive state. My gaze doesn't leave them though. I just stare, throwing in a sluggish blink every now and then.

Finally, they shift in their chairs, turning to face away from me and get back to their work. I have to stifle a chuckle when they both glance at me occasionally to make sure I'm not still staring at them.

Now, maybe I can get some work done.

When I first started college, I thought I wanted to be a weatherman. You know, the guy who stands in front of the green screen and makes terrible weather puns? At that time, I didn't realize most of them just report the weather, they aren't the ones who determine the forecast. By the time I learned I would have a better chance at that career with a journalism degree than a meteorology degree, I'd fallen in love with the science.

Weather is fascinating. Especially now, when climate change is affecting us and straining our ability to accurately predict the rapid changes. Now that I'm going to be able to afford to pursue a master's degree, I've shifted my focus more onto climatology. I'm not sure exactly what career I want in the field yet. Research is vital, but sounds a bit boring. The kid in me wants to be a storm chaser like my idol, Tim Samaras. Who knows? Maybe I'll find a way to do both.

I hit the books hard and don't even realize how much time has passed until my stomach starts sounding like an angry badger. No wonder, I've been here for over six hours. I'm not sure if I want to go home yet, or just grab something to eat and go to the gym. After packing up my books, I head out to the hallway and text Denton.

> **Me: Is the intervention over?**
> **Denton: Not yet.**
> **Me: How is it going?**
> **Denton: Brutal, man. But Kenny is stubborn as fuck.**
> **Me: Want to grab some food and hit the gym?**
> **Denton: Already ate, but I'll meet you at the gym. Half hour?**
> **Me: Okay**

I hit the drive thru at a local burger joint and scarf down a cheeseburger and fries while sitting in the gym parking lot. Shut up. I can't be the only one who has done that. I did get a particularly ugly look from a large guy on the way to his car. Might be the milkshake I'm sipping.

Denton nods at me from a treadmill, and I join him, claiming the next in the row and setting it to a brisk walk to warm up.

"I don't know how you do that," he gripes.

"Manage these good looks on a daily basis? All in the genes, nothing you can do about that."

Denton scoffs. "Eat all that heavy food and then work out. I'd puke."

"It's a gift." A few moments of silence pass before I tell him. "The girl standing by the water cooler is checking you out."

The hope drains from his face when he sees who I'm talking about. "No way, vapid personality and huge fake tits. I'm out."

"That bad, huh?" I increase my speed to a fast jog. "Tits don't look bad from here."

"Trust me, man. I took her sweater off and it looked like her nipples were trying to give me directions, but couldn't agree. Looked like one of those puffy eyed goldfish. My eyes crossed every time I saw them. And she couldn't hold a conversation that wasn't about gossip or fashion."

His gaze travels to the young woman working the desk, and I laugh. "Ah, you've already chosen your next victim."

"She's in my calc class and she's smart as hell. You know I like the smart ones." He increases his speed to match mine. "I had to pretend to be stuck on a problem to get her to help me. When she bent over my desk, she smelled amazing."

"That's not creepy at all."

"Says the guy who has unsuccessfully chased the same woman for two years."

"I'm winning her over," I reply with a shrug.

"Falling on your ass is a wonderful way to make an impression," he teases.

"I didn't tell you that so you could use it against me."

Denton laughs and turns his head to look at me. "Have we met, of course—"

And that is when karma comes in and knocks the hell out of him. My little roll in the mud is nothing to his spectacular display of athleticism. His phone slips out of his armband and crashes to the conveyor belt. He grabs for the phone between his feet, but it is instantly chucked behind him, and all he manages to do is throw himself off balance.

I reach over and hit the emergency stop on his machine, but it isn't fast enough. He falls onto his shoulder and is flung off the belt and onto the floor on top of his phone. A crunch sound says he either broke his phone or his arm.

Stopping my machine, I restrain my laughter and ask, "Are you okay?"

Denton leaps to his feet and scoops up his shattered phone. "I'm good." His eyes dart to search for the hot girl at the desk, but she's already on her way over to him. "Fuck," I hear him mumble, as she approaches.

"Are you okay?" she asks.

"Fine," Denton says. "Just…dropped my phone."

"And yourself," I add cheerfully.

The woman giggles and lays a hand on his arm. "It happens

at least once a day, and a phone is usually the culprit."

"Well, you taught the phone not to mess with you again," I remark, and he gives me a dirty look. I decide to take pity on him, and turn to the girl. "Hi, I'm Noble. It was actually my fault. I hit the emergency stop and I think that's what threw him off."

"Well, make sure you wear the clip," she tells him, with a pretty smile.

Denton starts chatting with her, and accompanies her back to the desk to fill out an accident report. When he returns, his expression is smug. "Got her number."

"If only you had a phone to store it."

"Fuck off," he laughs. "I was due for an upgrade. I'll shop for a new one tomorrow."

The apartment is quiet when we get home, and Kenny's parents are gone. Trey is lounging on the couch, watching a movie while Kenny broods in the recliner. Denton heads to the kitchen, retrieves a bag of French fries from the freezer, and drapes them over his shoulder before joining us in the living room.

"Do you think you need to get it checked out?" I ask, and he shakes his head.

"Nah, just bruised it good." He turns to Kenny. "So, what's up?"

"I want to throw a party tomorrow night," Kenny says. Wow. That intervention went well. He continues, "If I don't get my grades up by the end of the year and pass all my classes, my parents aren't going to pay my tuition or anything. I'll have to go back home and work in the linen factory like the rest of the rejects. So, I want to have one more rager, get drunk, and smash some strange before I have to stop for good."

His voice is sulky.

Denton sighs. "One, you don't have to stop for good or become celibate for fuck's sake. Just clean up your act until you get caught up, then it's all about moderation, like I said before. And two, I'm fine with a party as long as you stop acting like someone pissed in your Cheerios. Adulting isn't as bad as it seems."

"You seem to be doing a bang up job at it," Trey laughs, staring at Denton's arm. "What happened?"

"Noble shoved me off a treadmill," I hear him say as I head to my room.

Asshole.

An hour later, Kenny has emerged from his shitty mood, and we sit around playing the newest first person shooter. I like games, but Trey is obsessed. It's no surprise he's going to school to be a game designer. My phone beeps with a text from Jani.

Jani: I'll pick you up at six in the morning.
Me: Or we could just leave from here after you spend the night.

I can't resist baiting her. She never fails to give me shit.

Jani: Nah, I'm already naked in bed. Don't want to have to get up.
Me: Pic or isn't true.

My heart leaps in my chest when a text comes through that urges me to download a picture. Holy shit. She actually sent me—

A picture of her bare feet sticking out the end of the covers.

Me: Mmm...how did you know I have a foot fetish?

The amount of time it takes for her to respond makes me laugh. I can picture her trying to figure out if I'm serious or not.

Jani: Very funny. I almost fell for it.
Me: Fine, I'm not into feet. You have cute little toes though.
Jani: Omg. I'll see you in the morning.

Since I have to be up at the ass crack of dawn, I cut the video games short and go to bed.

It feels like I've just closed my eyes when my phone rings, and I slap at it until I hit the speaker button.

"Are you up?" Jani asks.

"Mmm Hmm."

"Liar," she laughs. "Get up and dress warm." She pauses for a moment. "Oh, and wear dark clothes, black if you can."

The floor is cold on my feet as I shamble over to turn on my light. "Are we robbing a bank?"

"You'll see," she teases. "I'll pick you up in a few minutes."

Fifteen minutes later, I'm climbing into her car. She's so peppy in the morning that I kind of want to slap her. A morning person, I'm not.

"Where are we going? It's still dark out," I mumble.

She picks up a coffee from her console and hands it to me. "Have you heard of urban exploration?"

She pulls out of our apartment complex as I sip the nectar of the gods. "Is that where people take pictures of abandoned buildings?"

Her grin lights up the car. "Some take pictures, but it's mostly just about exploring, seeing places most people don't get to see."

Holy shit. We are going to break into somewhere. I'm suddenly wide awake. "Okay, and how many years are we facing for this adventure?"

Her lips curl up and she gives me a sideways glance. "It's just a little trespassing, but if you don't want to…"

"No, I'm in." I have a clean record. Besides, trespassing usually just gets you chased off the property with a warning never to come back. Don't ask me how I know that. "What are we exploring?"

"Mid-State."

Is she serious? That place is creepy in the daytime. "The asylum?"

"Yep." She smirks at me. "You look a little worried. Afraid you'll find some relatives there?"

"I'm more concerned about the mutants that live in the basement." It's a well known story in town that a crazy doctor was experimenting on people and managed to make mutants, that they say still live in the basement of the abandoned building.

Jani bursts out laughing. "You don't really believe that."

"Okay, but when some three-eyed frog man with flippers attacks us, just remember I can run faster than you."

"I have a taser for crazy frog men." After parking behind the asylum, she opens her bag and damned if she doesn't carry a taser. "I've never been attacked by an amphibian before, but there are sometimes homeless people or junkies."

Before she can get out of the car, I grab her arm. "Tell me you don't ever do this alone."

"No, I always have backup. And today that's you." She leans over and presses her cold lips to mine. Am I really going to follow this chick into a dark, abandoned mental hospital that may or may not be home to some biological monstrosity?

Yep.

"Have you been in here before?" I ask.

She hands me a flashlight and slings a small bag onto her back. "Yeah, a couple of years ago. I didn't make it very far though. A bunch of teenagers were partying here and it kind of killed the mood."

"Okay, here's the deal. If I'm venturing into mutant territory, then you have to come to the party we're throwing at my apartment tonight."

Looking back over her shoulder, she throws me a smile and replies, "We'll see." Without any hesitation, she scrambles over the ten-foot-high, chain link fence that surrounds the property.

Damn, that was hot.

I follow her over, and we creep across the crumbling concrete parking lot, trying not to trip over the bottles and debris scattered around us.

We explore the back of the building, looking for an easy way in. The dock door is raised a few inches, and Jani pulls a short crowbar out of the bag. She pries open the door until it's high enough for us to lie down and roll under.

I go first, shining the light into the darkness to make sure I'm not going to come face to face with a rat…or worse. Once I'm inside, she rolls under the door, ignoring the filth that clings to her.

Her face betrays her excitement when she jumps to her feet. Our flashlights are more like powerful spotlights, and they push back the darkness just ahead of us. "The sun is just starting to rise, so it'll be lighter when we get into the hall," she remarks.

She pauses at the edge of a staircase. "We can go up and explore the patient wings, or down and prove that silly mutant story is a myth. Your choice."

"Up."

Giggling, she starts up the stairs, but I step ahead of her. If we run into anything crazy, I have no idea what I'll do since I don't have a weapon, but it's still instinct to keep her behind me.

"My white knight," she sighs, and I flip her off over my shoulder.

A door stands open on the first landing, and as Jani predicted, thin light filters through the dirty windows as the sun rises. The smell of decay and mold are so thick I feel like I can taste them.

We stay side by side, slowly making our way down the hall and there's so much to look at I don't know where to point my eyes first. Paint bubbles on some walls and hangs off of others in strips, showing the crumbling drywall beneath.

We pick our way around a pile of thin metal beams and foam panels; a chunk of the drop ceiling that has given way. Colorful graffiti lets us know we're far from the first people to check out this place. This actually is kind of cool.

Jani pauses by a door, then tugs it open. The loud screech it emits sends a shiver through me, but she just grins back at me. "Look, it's a padded room. Or it was."

Some kind of shredded material I don't recognize coats the walls of the tiny room. At some point there was probably a bed, but all that's left now is a wooden chair in the corner. A window the size of my hand lets in a narrow stream of light. "What a nightmare," I breathe. "Can you imagine being locked in here, only seeing the outside through that tiny window? I don't know how that would cure crazy. I'd go nuts."

"Me too." Jani runs her fingers over the stone windowsill. "This place was used as an orphanage first, then a TB hospital, before it became an asylum. It has quite a history."

"How long has it been closed down?"

"Almost fifty years. There's some disagreement over who holds the deed now so it can't be torn down or sold."

"Wow, you really did your homework."

"I always research first. That's half the fun," she says, and grabs my hand. "Come here, feel this."

She places my fingers on the windowsill, and I can feel the letters H and N carved into the stone. "It's stuff like this that's so interesting. Someone stood in this spot, locked in this little room, and carved their initials into the windowsill. Doesn't it make you wonder who they were? What they were thinking about or dreaming about? Where they are today, or if they're still alive?"

Stepping up behind her, I wrap my arms around her waist and rest my chin on her shoulder. "I never suspected you of being a romantic."

Her loud snort kills all thoughts of romance. "It's not romantic, you psycho!"

"I didn't mean it gave me a hard-on, for fuck's sake. I meant you're a dreamer, a sentimentalist. I like it."

"If you say so," she giggles.

We step back into the hall and make our way up another dark staircase. "It's the children's ward," she says.

"Okay, this is creepy," I whisper.

"Why are you whispering?" she whispers back.

"Mutants have super hearing."

Instead of separate patient rooms, this floor has a long, open area where rusted metal cribs and tarnished bed frames line the walls. A few broken toys lie scattered across the floor, waiting for half a century for little hands to bring them to life again.

"Why would they have babies or kids that young in an asylum?"

"I don't know," she replies, gazing around us. "It didn't take much to be thought insane back then. Maybe they were just special needs kids, you know, kids with Down Syndrome or Autism."

Well, that's depressing as fuck.

The next room reeks and it's apparent why once we shine our lights on the floor. Right in the center of the filthy tile is a huge fungal bloom the size of a kiddie wading pool. It's an odd pink color with black splotches here and there.

We both take a step back. "Yeah, let's go. We might get sick," Jani says.

"Or turn into inhuman creatures of the night," I add, leading the way back out into the hall.

"There's only one more level," Jani says, pointing her flashlight toward the staircase.

"Let's do it."

After a few steps, I realize I can't hear her breathing behind me anymore and I turn, assuming she's stopped to look at something. She's standing, frozen, half in a doorway, staring at me.

"January? What is it?"

Suddenly, she screeches, and her whole body is jerked inside.

For the first time in my life I know what the phrase "my heart is in my throat" really means. In my panic, it feels like I could puke it out and it'd go beating across the floor.

"Jani!" I run to the door, only a few feet away, but it seems like an eternity. Stepping inside, I can't see anything. It's just another padded cell.

Then something clamps onto my arm, and I shriek like an old lady. It takes me a second to realize Jani is holding my arm, laughing so hard she can't speak.

"I'm going to kill you!" I wheeze, trying to slow my heart back down to a speed not usually maintained by meth addicts. "I damn near pissed myself!"

That doesn't exactly quell her laughter. "You th-thought the mutants got me." She barely manages to get the words out between laughing fits.

"I thought something had you. You're going to pay for that." She squeals when I pinch her ass.

Wiping her eyes, she peeks out the window. "The sun is up. We should go."

Thank fuck.

"Are you pissed?" she asks, grabbing my hips and grinning up at me.

"Nope, but no whining when I pay you back." I drop a kiss on her lips.

"I never whine."

Maybe she doesn't whine, but the little smart ass hums the Teenage Mutant Ninja Turtles theme song all the way down the hall. When we get back to the first level, there's a room we didn't see before, so we duck inside for a quick look. It's an old office and the floor is covered in files and dusty paper.

"Looks like this room was spared the water damage," I remark, picking up a file. "Holy shit, this is a medical record. Look."

Jani joins me while I shine the light on the yellowed paper. "Samuel Forger, age sixteen, committed in nineteen fifty-nine for homoerogenous thoughts," she reads aloud.

"Holy hell, they used to lock you up for that?"

"Looks like it."

Before she can look through any more of the papers, I stick my hand out to pick up a stack still sitting on a shelf and that's when the mutant finally gets me.

A sharp, piercing pain darts through my hand and up my arm, and it takes a moment for me to realize there's a furry ball made of teeth and claws locked onto it.

"Noble!" Jani yells.

I'm too busy running around the room, smashing my hand into everything like the Hulk on a steroid binge to answer her. I knock an old desk over and it crashes into the door, slamming it shut and closing us inside the room.

"Hold it still!" Jani shouts, pointing the taser at it.

"No! Are you crazy? You'll—"

Now, I was going to say, "You'll hit me" but I didn't get the chance before she fires. A flash of white hot pain shoots up my arm and spreads through my body, dropping me to the floor. The monster finally lets go and runs into a large hole in the wall, snarling and hissing the entire way, but it barely registers in my mind as I try to shake off the feeling I've just been plugged into a socket like a Christmas light.

"Oh my god, Noble, are you okay?" Fear is clear in her voice as she kneels beside me. "I'm so sorry. I panicked. I thought I could hit it."

"I'm okay," I grunt, sitting up. Sure, I'm cool. I just feel like I've been stomped by an elephant while experiencing a full body Charlie horse. "It bit me."

"I saw it. I've never seen a raccoon do that!" She tentatively removes the barbs from the taser that thankfully hooked to my sleeve instead of my skin.

"Mutant raccoon," I mumble.

Ignoring that, she takes off her stocking hat and wraps it around my bleeding hand. "We've got to take you to the hospital. Come on."

She grabs the door handle and pulls it, but it doesn't move. After a few more tries, I step around her and give it my best. At least the raccoon chewed up my left hand and not my right. It doesn't matter though because the door is stuck shut.

The only windows in the room are far too small for either of us to climb through. I step back and shake my head. "We're stuck."

Jani's eyes widen. "I never should've brought you here. This is all my fault. I just thought it'd be fun and an adventure and now you're hurt and we can't get out and—"

"Whoa," I chuckle, pulling her against me with my good arm. "Don't freak out on me. I'll call the guys and they'll get us out."

"Then the hospital."

"Then my doctor," I correct. "It's barely bleeding. Not an emergency."

"Then I'm going to suck your dick like it has chocolate filling to make this up to you," she babbles, making me laugh as I call Denton.

Denton isn't quite as amused about being woken up early to break into an insane asylum and rescue us, but he promises that he and the guys are on their way. Jani takes the phone and explains exactly how to get in and where we are. After she hangs up, all we can do is wait.

We sit on the floor and read through some of the files, though very few are still legible, until we hear footsteps in the hall. "Down here!" I call out.

Jani steadily taps on the door until Denton taps back. "You in there, man?"

"Yes, the door is jammed or something!"

The door rattles as they try with no luck to get it open. "Dude, just let me smash it," Trey says.

"Fine. You guys hear that? Get way back. Tons-of-fun is going to knock it down."

Jani and I retreat to the back wall. The first try only moves it a few inches, but it's quickly followed by a screech of metal across tile as Trey charges through it like a rhino. Slipping on the files, he falls on his ass and jumps back to his feet with comical speed for a man his size.

Pride fills his face as he smiles and announces, "Spoiler alert! I'm drunk."

"Good to know," I laugh.

"Thank you," Jani tells him. "Are you hurt?"

Trey looks at his arms and legs. "Not that I can tell. Ask me again tonight." He grins at her. "I did have to walk away from nailing this chick to come and help you, though."

"Yeah, sorry about that," Jani replies, rolling her eyes.

He flaps a hand at her. "S'okay. She had these long dreads. Having her on top was like going through a car wash."

"What happened to your hand?" Denton asks as we make our way back out of the building.

"A mutant got me."

"In the basement?"

"Oh, for fuck's sake," Jani groans. "There are no mutants."

"It was disguised as a raccoon."

"You probably need a rabies shot, then," Denton points out.

"Yeah, I'll call when we get home." Grinning down at Jani, I whisper in her ear. "So, about that party tonight."

Chapter Four

January

"I can't believe you're going to a Frat Hell party," Cassidy giggles, packing a plush teddy bear into a box.

"The guy got bitten by a raccoon because of me and had to have rabies shots. After I tased him. It was kind of hard to say no."

"Are you going to fuck him?"

"At the party, surrounded by a bunch of drunk idiots? No."

Wyatt walks into the room, and gives Cassidy a look. She turns to me. "So, we have something to talk to you about."

My hands slam onto my hips. "Did you knock her up already?"

"No!" Cassidy exclaims as Wyatt laughs.

He takes a seat across from me. "I want to offer you the general manager position at Scarlet Toys."

What? My head turns to Cassidy so quick my neck cracks. "Are you quitting?"

Adoring eyes sweep over Wyatt, and I get a brief pang in my stomach. What they have is something special. Something I really hope is waiting for me in the future. "I'm going to spend more time helping at the community center and I've opened a little online store to sell my plush animals. Wyatt talked me into giving it a go."

I force a smile. No matter how much I don't want to lose her at the store, she's happy, and I need to be happy for her. "That's amazing, Cass. Your animals are beautiful."

"Thanks, I don't expect it to be all that popular, but I'd like to keep it small, anyway. Offer special orders, monogramming etc." She waves her hand. "But I can't leave the store short-handed. You know my job backward and forward. You'll have to hire your replacement, but I can help with that if you want."

It's a great opportunity. More money for the same amount of hours, but more flexibility in my schedule. "When do you want me to start?"

Wyatt gets to his feet. "We'll run an ad this week for the job opening. After we get the new hire trained, you can take over. If you're accepting the position."

"Never found a position I wasn't cool with," I reply, and Cass rolls her eyes at me. "Yeah, I'm accepting." I hold up a finger before Wyatt can reply. "On one condition. You cannot keep Cassidy all to yourself. I know she's awesome and all that, but she was mine first. I want full bestie benefits. That means at least one girl's night per month, and I reserve the right to call her anytime I need to, and you can't prevent me from talking to her."

"Why would I do that?" Wyatt asks, amused.

"Ha! I've heard all about your…distracting member. Bestie trumps sex. Chicks before dicks. That's all I'm saying."

Wyatt looks at Cass. "Is she serious?"

Cass pulls her legs up until she's sitting cross legged. "Absolutely. And I agree. Ovaries before broveries."

Wyatt stares at us like we're both insane. "Broveries?"

Giggling, I suggest, "Uteruses before duderuses?"

Wyatt shakes his head and mutters something about crazy women as he leaves the room.

Cass looks me in the eye. "Seriously, though, Jani. I know I'm not around as much, but I'm still here whenever you need me."

Sighing, I reply, "Then tell me I'm completely crazy for letting things get this far with Noble. Because if someone doesn't talk me out of it, I'm going to fuck that guy like his dick is the key to happiness."

"It might be. Not his dick, specifically, but him. You never know. I'm happier now than I ever was, and while his cock definitely plays its role, it's the everyday things with Wyatt that make me happy."

"Ugh." I fall back on the couch. "You're not helping. Fine, I'll see how tonight goes and maybe I'll give his cock a little play time."

Wyatt retreats from the doorway. "I always manage to walk in at the wrong moment," he grumbles.

Cass and I break into laughter. "It's cute that he thinks there's ever a right moment when we're talking."

Cass giggles, looking toward the now empty doorway. "He's learning."

I can hear the party at Frat Hell before I get there. It's not that the music is all that loud, but the laughing and talking spill out of the windows they've opened to vent the pot smoke. Noble must have been waiting on me to show up because he yanks the front door open before I can knock.

"Hey, beautiful." He wastes no time pulling me in for a kiss. "You're just in time to watch me kick some ass at beer pong. Want to play?"

I'm going to need some alcohol to get through this night. "Sure, why not?"

His arm wraps around my waist as we head inside. Denton is sitting on the couch along with a group of other guys, all staring at the T.V.

"Dude! How did you miss him? Give me that!" One of the guys I don't recognize grabs the controller from the other, and takes over playing the shooting game.

Another grins up at me, either oblivious to the fact that Noble's arm is around me or too drunk to give a shit. "Heeey, sweet thing." Slurring like crazy, so it's definitely the latter. "Want to go home with me? I got something for you. It's ten inches long, full of sperm, and makes all the ladies scream."

Noble's face hardens, and he takes a step toward the guy, but I get between them. I've never needed anyone to fight my battles. "I'm not interested in seeing the sock under your bed."

A chorus of "ohh, buurn" fills the room. Before it ends, and the guy says something that's most likely going to lead to Noble beating his ass—judging by the look on Noble's face—I smile and start toward the kitchen.

"Sorry," Noble apologizes as soon as he catches up with me. "Scott is a dick. Want a shot?" He holds out a shot of Fireball, and I down it before taking another.

"Didn't bother me." I grin up at him. "Are we playing or what?"

The game is set up on a long, fold out table in the kitchen. The usual kitchen table has been relegated to a corner, where it holds an array of drinks and snacks.

We watch as a ball bounces into the last cup, and the winning team cheers. The losing team of guys both grumble and start stripping off their clothes. "Losers have to strip down to underwear for an hour," Noble explains.

Alarm bells start ringing in my head. Abort Mission! Retreat! "If you think I'm stripping down to panties in a houseful of drunken—"

"No." Noble practically barks the word. "No way are any of these guys seeing your panties when I haven't even seen them yet. We won't play by that rule."

If I didn't know any better, I'd say that expression on his face is jealousy. I pat his cheek with my hand and drop a quick kiss on his lips. "What makes you think I'm wearing any panties?"

His eyes nearly fall out of his head, then find their way to my leggings covered back side. Trey has to call his name twice before he shakes himself out of it. "Dude, quit ogling your girl's ass and get over here."

Kenny sets up the cups and pours in some beer. "All right, Broski, you two are up first."

Noble stares at Kenny. "Oh no, did you get hit with—"

"Yes," Kenny interrupts, shaking his head. "Fuckin Trey the bromosapien hit me with the bro card when I lost the last game."

I'm probably going to be sorry for asking. "What is a bro card?"

"If you get the bro card, every sentence you speak has to include a word with bro in it," Trey explains, handing me a ping pong ball. "And it can't just be bro. You have to mix it up."

Of course. Makes perfect sense.

"For how long?"

Noble grins down at me. "Whoever gives the card is the only one who can revoke it. So, whenever that happens, or the next morning, whichever comes first."

I toss the ball and hit one of Trey and Kenny's cups. Noble does the same, and we grin at them as they drink. "If we win this one, will you revoke the card, Brosicle?" Kenny asks.

"Yep. But it's not looking good so far."

A few turns later, Noble and I are killing it. Godzilla couldn't have done a better job of destroying them. "I'm kind of thirsty. Could I get a beer?" I ask, taunting them with the fact I've barely had to drink.

Laughing, Noble grabs a beer from a nearby cooler and hands it to me. "Watching you teach my friends a lesson is incredibly hot."

"Beginner's luck," I reply with a shrug.

Trey and Kenny both gape at me. "You've never played this game before?" Trey asks.

"Nope." He mumbles something that sounds a bit like *this some bullshit*, but I can't be sure.

I hit my next throw, but Noble's bounces back out. "Get it together, buddy." I shove him and attempt to retreat around the edge of the table.

"It's your fault," he announces. I'm pulled back against him, and his lips run up my neck before I feel his breath in my ear. "All I can think about is whether you're wearing panties or not."

"So if I told you I'm wearing black, lace boy shorts, would

that help?"

His groan makes me laugh. Maybe it's the alcohol, but I'm actually having fun. Noble's friends may be a little silly, but, hell, Cassidy and I act stupid together all the time.

We're down to the last cup, and Noble hands me the ball. "Come on, baby, you can do it."

The way Kenny stares at the cup and holds his breath makes it hard not to laugh, and I'm tempted to miss one more time just to draw it out. Instead, I toss it and it lands perfectly in the cup.

"Fuck," Kenny curses, quickly adding, "-ing brotastic."

Trey shakes his head, a wicked grin on his face, when Kenny turns to him, pleading, "Rematch?"

"No way. I'll take the card back at midnight."

"How the hell am I supposed to get a bro-job while talking like this?"

Noble and I both crack up at the way he slipped the word in that time. "Dude, Carl is in the living room if that's what you're looking for," Noble says.

His bottom lip sticks out in a pout that matches his sulky tone. "Fuck off, you know I'm not gay, Bro-ble."

That does it. I'm sure the alcohol is the main reason I fall into hysterics at the sound of Noble's modified name, but either way, it's hilarious. Noble's smile is wide and genuine as he watches me try to stifle the giggles that just won't quit. Listening to Trey and Kenny insult each other really doesn't help.

"This is bullshit, brotato. Just because you look like a *before* picture for Weight Watchers doesn't mean I should have to go without."

Trey slaps his considerable belly. "My gut can't compete with my dick, so there's no shortage of women who want to ride the Trey Train. Unlike you, not all of us want to expose ourselves to various strains of the hepatitis alphabet."

"But this is my last night to do this, bromosexual." He does a little stompy dance like a obstinate three year old, and I have to swallow back a laugh.

Trey finally takes pity on him. Or he's sick of hearing him

whine, I'm not sure which, but he sighs, "Fine. I revoke the bro card. Go give some poor girl three minutes of missionary, under the covers disappointment."

Kenny slaps him on the back and races off like pussy might have an expiration date.

"Can we step outside and get some air?" I ask, a few giggles still slipping through.

"Sure, we've got a fire burning out there." His dimple pops out, setting another fire alight.

My phone beeps and I give it a quick look. I recently posted an ad on the internet about the ring we found in the river, and now someone is trying to claim it.

The text reads: **I bought Mayetta that ring and I'd like it back.**

Wow, way to be nice about it, buddy. I may have believed him if he had spelled her name correctly.

Me: Sure, just let me know what the inscription says, as the ad requested.

I tuck the phone away, not interested in calling out this person's bullshit. I'm much more concerned with the sexy man in front of me and the feelings he's stirring up.

Turns out I lied to Cassidy. I am most definitely going to sleep with him in a house full of his friends tonight. It's that or drag him back to my apartment where my mother can hear, so, Frat Hell sex it is.

I grab my coat while Noble heads off to get his. He returns with a fluffy throw blanket and drapes it around my shoulders. "Oh!" Denton exclaims as he walks past. "She gets the binky? No one can touch the binky!"

Noble glares at him, which draws a smirk from Denton. "His baby blanket. He carries it around the house and no one is allowed to touch it."

Noble flips him off. "It's not a damned baby blanket. And no one touches it because you guys dirty up everything. I don't want it full of joint burns and soaked in Trey's sweat."

"It is really soft," I remark, pulling it around me. It smells good too, like him. "Thanks."

A few guys sit by the fire out back, passing a joint and talking about fixing a car. Noble drags an oversized Adirondack chair to the other side of the fire, then pulls me into his lap.

"I'm going to squish you," I protest.

He scoffs and spreads the blanket over us. "You're tiny."

"You obviously haven't met thunder and lightning." I clench one thigh and then the other to introduce them.

His eyes close briefly and he shakes his head at me, a small smile on his face. "I plan to make their acquaintance very soon."

His body is warm, and I snuggle into him. His arms wrap around my waist, under the blanket, and his hands rest on my thigh. "Do you have to work tomorrow?" he asks, nuzzling his chin into my neck.

"No, in a few weeks I'll be able to set my own hours, though. I'm replacing Cassidy as GM of Scarlet Toys."

He pinches my chin and turns my head toward him. "You got promoted to GM?"

"Yep. Cass just told me."

A soft kiss lands on my lips. "Congratulations. That's great."

He can be so sweet sometimes. I settle back against his chest. "Thanks. I hate to lose Cass, but I'm happy to take the job."

His fingers curl into my hair, playing with it. "I'm sure you two will still hang out."

"Yeah, what about you? You graduate this year, don't you?" I hadn't really thought about it until now, but he'll likely move after school. Now that I like him, I hate to think how temporary this might be.

"With my bachelor's degree, yes, but I won a scholarship to continue to my master's degree."

Hope leaps in my chest. "Here? At the same school?"

"Yes." He grins down at me. "Why, were you hoping to escape me at the end of the year?"

I run my hand up and down his thigh. "Nah, I kind of like you."

"Kind of?" He slides his hand to tickle my ribs with his fingertips.

"As long as you don't tell anyone." I tilt my head up and bring my lips to his. "Congratulations on the scholarship. What do you do with a master's in weather?"

"In meteorology and climatology," he corrects. "I'm not exactly sure what line of work I want to end up in. Maybe research. My focus has shifted more to the study of climate change." He grins. "But storm chasing is a real possibility."

"Mmm...storm chasing. That's kind of sexy. I've always wanted to see a tornado, but if I ever did, I'd probably pass out or wet myself." Yeah, Jani, that's how you do it. Just keep up all that sexy talk. Ugh, sometimes I wonder who thought it would be a good idea to put me in charge of a vagina.

My talk of involuntary urination doesn't seem to faze him though. His hand sweeps across my ribs, and I reach under the blanket to unbutton my coat. Taking it as the invitation I meant it to be, he runs his warm palm across my breast, cupping it, then running a thumb over my nipple.

"I feel like I'm sixteen again, getting felt up under a blanket," I whisper, before claiming his cool lips with mine.

"I was never this lucky at sixteen. Beautiful woman in my arms, all soft and sweet," he murmurs, kissing me again.

We're interrupted by Trey's loud cry. "Look! It's a UFO!"

I had practically forgotten they were there. At some point, Trey and Denton have joined the fun. Right now, five drunk men are staring at the sky. I'm overcome with a brief moment of evilness when I picture how funny it'd be if a bird flew over and shit right now, since their mouths are all hanging open like an inflatable sex doll.

"I don't see anything," one of them argues. I don't recognize him, so he must not be from the circle.

"Right there!" Trey insists, stumbling to his feet and pointing at the sky. He takes a quick step back, catching his balance.

It's funny, because one of the things I discovered the first time I drank was that looking up at the stars is not a good idea. Everything spins, and you want to puke.

Denton snorts and takes a drink of his beer. "That's a

satellite, you idiot."

"Is not! It's a UFO. Maybe aliens."

Another guy speaks up. "I saw a UFO before. 'Bout three years ago."

"See," Trey says, vindicated, pointing to the sky again like we might have forgotten where it was. "It's a UFO."

"Lots of things are UFO's if you're stupid," Denton says.

Noble nuzzles my neck. "You want to go to my room? Unless you're invested in the alien debate."

Getting to my feet, I wrap the blanket back around my shoulders. "Let's go."

"Nice angle on your dangle, there, dude!" Denton yells as we walk past, and Noble flips him off.

"He's just mad because I made the new neighbor think he's gay."

Laughing, I grab his hand. "Let's go put the dangle to good use."

He doesn't have a response for that.

Noble's room is neat and pretty much looks like you'd expect any young guy's bedroom to look, except for the massive poster of a tornado on one wall, and another that depicts the patterns of ocean currents.

I'm trying to make some sense out of the ocean poster when he presses his chest to my back. "Most people don't realize how much of our weather, especially temperature, is controlled by ocean currents. With the ice caps melting, they dump freshwater into the stream which affects the density and alters the flow."

It occurs to me that Noble may be smarter than I gave him credit for. The passion he has for his field shines through in his voice. He certainly isn't the party all the time slacker I thought he was. He works hard and has plans for his future. I feel bad I rushed to judgment just based on how he goofs off with his friends.

"Like in that disaster movie where New York freezes instantly?"

Chuckling, he kisses my neck. "They exaggerated the hell out of it, but that's the scenario it's based on. Realistically, it could take two centuries to affect it to a dangerous extent."

"Mmm." I tilt my head, giving him better access. "Talk science to me, nerd boy."

"Barometric pressure," he whispers, reaching around to caress my breasts. "Evapotranspiration, southern oscillation—"

I stop his words with my mouth, grinning at the sound he always makes when I slip my tongue against his. Still kissing me, he reaches past me to lock his door.

"Do you have a condom?" I ask, unbuttoning his pants.

Maybe he didn't think I was actually going to sleep with him, because his lips fall open a little, and it takes him a second to answer. "Yeah, in the night stand."

Rough hands slide up my sides, taking my shirt with them. His lips return to mine, and I'm so lost in the kiss I don't notice he's unclipped my bra until the cool air chills my nipples. Deep blue eyes delve into mine when we break apart, and his voice is firm when he says, "Do you have any idea how much I want to fuck you? All I've thought about is having you squirming under my tongue while I make you come."

Heat races across my skin at his words, and he smiles. "You like me talking dirty to you." It's not a question, and I don't bother with a response.

We strip each other, pausing to kiss and lick and caress until we're both out of our minds with desire. My back arches as he sucks my nipple, and I explore the muscles of his back, reveling in the way they flex under my fingers.

I love his body, the smooth skin, sprinkled lightly with hair in all the right places. Lean and muscled, warm and hard. It's perfect. When he slides a thick finger inside me, then another, I spread my legs wider, and reach for his cock. I wrap my hand around it, delighting in the weight of it on my palm and the little breath he takes when I stroke the silky, hot skin.

"You're so wet," he murmurs.

I'm also close to coming already. "Condom," I gasp, my ability to speak in coherent sentences temporarily stalled by the movement of his fingers.

Flashing me a wicked grin, his lips scorch a trail of kisses down my stomach as he moves out of my reach, wrapping his arms around my thighs. "Noble, you don't have to—"

The unfinished sentence hangs in the air, punctuated by my loud moan. His hot tongue moves over my clit in slow, tight circles, and my hands clamp onto his hair. Holy fuck, the man has skills. My legs start to tremble, and I feel reality slipping away as I'm overcome by sensation. "Noble, please, oh god."

A little growl rumbles his chest, making his mouth vibrate against me, and it's the last thing I feel before falling into a long, pulsing, orgasm. His fingers and tongue work to draw it out until every inch of me is buzzing and alive.

He crawls up my body, and I caress his cock again. I swear it's even harder than before, swollen and hot. I barely have a moment to lick just under the head when he pulls away with a gasp. "Not this time, babe. I want to be inside you."

He sits back against the headboard and rolls on a condom. I straddle him before he can protest, and his head falls back as I sink down on him. He's thick and just long enough so he fills me completely without trying to split me in half, but it still takes a moment to adjust to him.

His hands hold my hips, and I kiss along his jaw, moving to his neck and ear. His whole body goes lax when I lick his earlobe. Hmm...good to know.

I take it nice and easy, teasing him with long, slow movements. "January," he moans, "you feel so fucking good."

Grabbing the headboard, I start to fuck him with determination. We're both panting and covered in sweat when he rolls us over so he's on top and pounds into me like a madman. I love to see him lose all control like this, and the thought shoves me into another shattering orgasm. I look up at him as his eyes squeeze shut and his mouth falls open, his body trembling against mine.

We stay right like that, his body sprawled over mine for a long minute, just basking in the sensations we've created together. I've always enjoyed sex, but it's never been anything like this. We have some serious chemistry together.

Finally, he plants one last soft kiss on my lips and sits up.

Staring down, his eyes widen, and he warns, "Uh…don't freak out."

Not the words I want to hear right after a guy pulls out of me. "The condom came off."

"What? It came off! When?"

"I don't know! The damn things are tight enough to strangle it, I've never had one come off!"

I sit up, and we both look around the bed frantically until the only other place it could be becomes clear. "Great," I grumble, sticking my fingers inside myself to try to locate the wayward condom. Have you ever tried to find a slick piece of rubber when everything is wet? It's like trying to grab a grape in a bowl of Jell-O. Freaking impossible.

When I look up, frustrated, Noble is staring at me, and not just with his eyes. "Seriously? This turns you on?"

"Babe, you're wet and fingering yourself on my bed. This is all I'm going to be able to think about until I die."

Glaring at him, I gesture between my legs. "You want to help?"

A snort of laughter escapes me at the way he leaps across the bed. I barely get the words out and he's grinning at me. "I was afraid you'd never ask."

His fingers are gentle when they slip inside, feeling and searching. "I don't feel anything," he murmurs.

"I think that's my line," I giggle, and he deliberately rubs across my G spot, making me gasp.

"Uh-huh. That's what I thought," he says with a smirk. A few more seconds pass before he adds, "I can't find it."

As tempted as I am to point out that's my line as well, I refrain. "It's got to be there. It's a vagina, not a bottomless pit! And I am not going to the hospital for an emergency condom extraction!"

After a few long minutes, he sighs. "I swear there's nothing in you."

Before I can argue again, he grins and says, "Uh…Jan? It's stuck to your ass cheek." His hand slides under me to lift my ass off the bed, and I feel it peel away. Ew.

I rarely get embarrassed, but this is not the way I picture a first time with anyone. I cover my hot face with my hands.

Noble chuckles and pulls my hands away. "Come on, don't get all girly on me just because we had to do a little spelunking."

"Oh my god, shut up," I laugh, reaching for my panties.

"What do you think you're doing?" he asks, pushing me down onto my back again.

"Well, walking naked through an apartment full of guys doesn't sound appealing, so I'm getting dressed."

Pinning my arms to the bed, he grins down at me. "Where are you planning to go?"

"Call me crazy, but my plan is to go home. You know, the place I live?"

His head dips, and he runs his tongue across my nipple. "I have an attached bathroom and that's as far as you get to go. I'm not through with you. Not even close."

The little moan I utter makes his lips tilt up. "I don't know. Do you have some duct tape so we can keep the condom on this time? Or maybe some super glue."

Pausing for a second, he asks, "Do we need to get you a morning after pill?"

"I'm on the shot, so I'm covered. Do I need to get tested or anything?"

"Nope, I'm clean."

"We're still going to use condoms," I tell him.

"I wasn't suggesting otherwise. Now, turn over so I can make you beg me some more."

My mouth drops open. "I didn't beg!" I did. I distinctly remember pleading with him not to stop.

He grabs my hips and flips me over, covering my body with his. Brushing my hair aside, he delivers little sucking kisses on the back of my neck. His voice is high as he says, "Oh, yes, Noble, don't stop. You have the best cock in the universe. It's so massive and hard and perfect. I can't live another second without it. Sound familiar?"

Okay, now he's full of shit. "You must be thinking of someone else."

"Never. You're all I've thought about for too damn long, January. Now, I want to make sure you can't stop thinking about me."

Over the next few hours, he proves his point, searing the night into my memory as the best sex I've ever had.

Noble's scent wafts over me when I drag my eyes open, groaning at the wonderful way my body aches, but he's not in bed beside me. I must've been out of it not to hear him get up. I usually sleep really light, but I guess mind blowing orgasms will do that for a girl.

Thankfully, the rest of the guys are nowhere to be seen when I creep out of Noble's bedroom. After all the drinking last night, I'm not surprised. Their beds probably won't see the end of them until at least noon. Pulling my hair up into a messy ponytail, I walk into the kitchen and stop dead in my tracks.

Noble stands at the stove, dressed only in a pair of boxers, his back to me as he flips sausages in a frying pan. His hips swish back and forth as he belts out his own version of Despacito.

I wanted to make an omelet with pico.

But there's no eggs cause Denton's too damn cheapo.

He throws in a few pelvic thrusts, and shakes his ass.

So I'll just make sausage burritos.

I swallow back a laugh as he tosses a fork in the sink, and slides back over to the stove, singing.

In the sinko.

"Do you take requests?" I ask, and he jumps, turning to face me. A smile climbs across his face.

"Is the request for me to stop singing?" There's not a scrap of embarrassment on his face.

"No, you're a natural. Obviously very fluent."

He crosses his arms and leans against the counter. The muscles in his abdomen tighten, reminding me of how they flexed when he was on top of me last night.

"All you have to do is add O to translate a word to Spanish," he says. "Not many people know that."

I grab a bottle of water from the fridge. "I'll try to keep it in mind."

Grabbing my arm, he pulls me against him and nuzzles my neck. "Did you have fun last night?"

"You mean at the party or after?" He's so much fun to tease.

"At the party. Your cries of ecstasy and pleads for me not to stop made it pretty clear you enjoyed the after."

He grins down at me when my arms circle his neck, and I plant a quick kiss on his lips. "I did have fun. Your friends are crazy, but they make me laugh."

"So, let's see, you have fun with me, you like my friends, and you worship my cock like a pagan god. I think that all adds up to you being my girlfriend."

His words take a second to sink in and then I'm not sure what to say. He has definitely caught me off guard. "You don't think it's a little…soon," I stall.

He shrugs and runs a palm down my back, resting his hand on the swell of my ass. "I know what I want, and she's standing right in front of me, looking terrified." He threads his fingers through my hair. "Tell me what you're afraid of."

I can't believe the words fall out of my mouth. "That I'll get serious and you won't. I'll get my heart broken and you'll move onto the next girl." Wow, way to just blurt those issues out.

"Has that happened to you before?" His voice is soft as he plays with my hair.

"No, not me…someone I care about. It nearly killed her."

It's not something I like to talk about, but I've watched my mother spend her whole life alone after my dad ran out on her. She always swore she was over him, that she could never love a man who abandoned her kid, and I believe that, but it also meant she wouldn't trust a man again either.

His sky blue eyes are intense when they stare into mine. "I can't predict the future or where this will lead us any more than you can, beautiful. But I can promise you I'm serious about us. I love spending time with you and I want to know that you feel the same."

"I do," I murmur. "I have a lot of fun with you."

"I want to be able to tell people you're mine."

Stepping back, I grin up at him. "Staking your claim, huh?"

"That's right."

"Okay," I sigh, as if he's really putting me out. "I'll be your girlfriend."

His face lights up and he slams his lips to mine, kissing me until I feel half drunk with it. "Okay, here are the stipulations. One, I need a daily blow job. Two, I need daily access to your vagina, both orally and—."

Denton steps into the room, interrupting. "Dude, shut up. My head is going to explode."

"I have a girlfriend," Noble tells him with a goofy smile. He sounds like a twelve year old boasting to his friends.

Denton grabs a carton of orange juice out of the fridge and nods at me as he walks by. "My condolences."

"He's just jealous," Noble taunts, returning to his cooking. The sausages are burnt black when he flips them over.

"Smooth," Denton remarks. "Maybe it's because you weren't singing to them."

A snort of laughter escapes me as I sit across the table from Denton. "Do you always sing while you cook?"

"Of course. When the big record labels come calling, I have to be ready."

"Good thinking."

Dropping the burnt sausage in the trashcan, he turns to me, "Do you want to grab breakfast at the diner?"

"An orgasm and waffles? You sure know how to treat a girl. I'm going to use your bathroom real quick first."

Trey walks out of Noble's bathroom just as I walk through his room. He nods at me, so I don't think anything of it. Kenny must be in the hall bathroom. I relieve myself, wash my hands and meet Noble back in the kitchen. It isn't until Noble drops me off after breakfast, so he can get some studying done, that things get weird.

Mom lies on the couch, watching television, but she mutes it the second I walk in. "Well, look at you, staying out all night. How scandalous."

"Very funny." I flop onto the couch next to her. "What are we watching?" Wincing, I shift around a little. My ass cheek is sore for some reason. Maybe Noble scratched me or something.

"It's about a group of people who live in Alaska. See those guys, they're hunting a moose."

Fascinating. Shit, both cheeks are starting to burn, What the hell? Trying to ignore it, I turn to Mom.

"How are you feeling?" She was diagnosed about five years ago with multiple sclerosis. She's not wheelchair bound, but it does limit her mobility. She worked for years at a plastics factory, but as soon as they found out she was sick, they fired her. She got a year of unemployment insurance out of them, but that was all. After twenty years of working for them, they used some lame excuse that she was late too often and not dedicated to the job, to get rid of her. She gets disability payments now, but it's not nearly enough to live on, especially since some of her treatments aren't covered by her disability insurance. So, she lives with me.

"Had a little dizziness today, but otherwise not bad. I was thinking of making some chicken and dumplings for dinner."

A yawn jumps from my throat, and I stretch my screaming muscles. The burn of my ass is only growing. I need to go to my room and see what the crazy guy has done to me. "Mmm, sounds good. I think I'll take a nap. Cass is coming by later."

Mom grins at me. "That boy wore you out, huh?"

"Mom!"

"I like him, Jani. He seems like a sweet kid. And he's obviously crazy about you."

"Of course." I drop a kiss on her cheek. "I look like my mom."

"Are you sucking up so I'll make homemade rolls to go with it?"

"You know me too well."

As soon as I'm alone in my room, I yank down my pants and underwear, and look at my ass in the mirror. It looks perfectly normal, not even red. Which makes no sense because it feels like I've been paddled for hours. I try to think back to the night before. I wasn't drunk. I remember everything.

The condom stuck to my butt cheek, but that wouldn't set it on fire, and both are in agony now. I grab a washcloth and my phone and retreat to the bathroom. I dial Noble, then put it on speaker while I wet the cloth with cold water. I don't see anything, but it feels like it's burning so water seems like a good option.

"Miss me already?" Noble says without a hello.

"What the hell did you do to me?"

"What? What are you talking about?"

"My ass! You did something to my ass! It's like it's been dipped in lava!"

"I didn't do anything. I—oh fuck. Trey!" he screams, and then all I can hear is raised voices until he returns. "Baby, I'm so sorry."

I rub the dripping wet cloth across my ass, sighing at the relief just as he says, "Whatever you do, don't put water on it. It makes it worse. Trey tried to prank me by putting capsaicin cream on my toilet seat."

Yeah.

Too fucking late.

The surface of the sun couldn't compete with my poor butt cheeks right now.

"I'm going to fucking kill him! Oh god, it burns. What do I do?"

"Milk," Noble replies, trying to hide the amusement in his voice.

"Are you laughing? Are you fucking laughing right now when my ass has turned into Krakatoa?"

"No, I swear—"

A knock at the door interrupts us. "Jani, are you okay?" Mom asks.

Of course, because I'm shrieking like a banshee.

"I'm fine!" I call out, before lowering my voice to talk to Noble. "If you know a way to stop this you'd better tell me or so help me, your balls are next!"

"Milk," he says again. "I'm serious. It won't stop it completely, but it'll make it bearable. Then you just have to wait for it to wear off."

Great. Fantastic. Mom knocks again. "Jani, what's going on?"

Fuck it. "Can you bring me the milk?"

"Milk?"

"Yes, milk. Please hurry."

Mom enters carrying a half gallon of milk, looking at me like I've completely lost it when she sees me standing in the shower, naked from the waist down. "What the hell, Jani? What were you yelling about?"

I snatch the milk and pour it over my ass, making sure to get every inch, reveling in the instant cooling effect. "It's Noble's fault," I snap, when I realize she's gaping at me. I mean, fair enough, it's not the most normal thing to do.

"Hey, I didn't do it!"

Shit. I forgot I still had him on speaker. "I'll call you back." I reach over and hit the disconnect button.

"Trey put Capsaicin cream on the toilet to prank Noble, but I sat on it," I explain to mom, glaring at her when she bursts out laughing.

"Aren't you going to rinse off the milk?"

"No, water isn't my friend right now."

I can hear her laugh echoing through the house as I wrap a towel around me and stalk to my room, flopping onto my stomach on the bed where I plan Trey's eventual disembowelment.

Chapter Five

Noble

I'm walking on air when I head to my classes after my weekend with Jani. I finally have the girl I've wanted for so long, and after this semester, I won't have to worry about making tuition payments anymore, so I'll actually be able to take her out to nice places.

I'm barely through the classroom door when Mr. Fields, my advisor, pops his head through the door. "Noble, do you have a minute?"

Mr. Fields waves at my advanced algebra teacher, and she nods at us, turning toward the board to start her lecture, one I am only too happy to miss. I grab my book bag and follow Mr. Fields to his office, crossing my fingers there hasn't been some problem with the scholarship money.

"Are you still working for the supercenter?" he asks as we take a seat in his office.

Oh no. I can't possibly be over income or something can I?

"Yes, part time after class and some weekends."

"Well, I got a call from WFUK and it seems their intern quit. They're looking for someone else to fill the paid internship position until the end of the term. There's a possibility of continuing to work for them next year too, if everything goes well. They usually take a broadcasting student, but since you're studying to be a meteorologist, I suggested you as a replacement. Is that something you'd be interested in?"

Is he kidding? I know a rare opportunity when I see one. "I...I'm definitely interested. Thanks for recommending me."

"I assume you have some questions," he says, leaning back in his chair.

"I assume I do too, but my mind is blank right now. You have no idea how happy I'd be to get out of that meat department."

Mr. Fields chuckles and shakes his head. He has been my advisor for almost four years now and he's a cool guy. He's never treated me like an unfortunate poor kid and has always been around when I needed advice. He's easy to talk to and seems to genuinely love his job.

"They pay twelve dollars an hour, and they'll work around your school schedule. It generally ranges from fifteen to twenty hours per week." He slides a paper packet across the table. "If you accept, they'd like you to start after the holidays. That should allow you to give the supercenter enough notice, right?"

"Screw them." The words pop out of my mouth before I can stop them, and I feel the blood drain from my face. "Sorry! I didn't mean to say that out loud."

Mr. Fields throws back his head and people down the hall can probably hear his booming laugh. "No worries, kid. I worked retail when I was young. No amount of money could make me do it again."

"What do I need to do?" I flip through the packet he handed me.

"Just read through that, fill out the paperwork, and show up at the time and date on the last sheet."

Standing, I reach to shake his hand. "Thank you so much. I can't wait to get started."

"Stop in and let me know how it's going," he says, and I agree.

Once I'm in the hall, I have no intention of going back to Algebra. I'm going to do something I very rarely do—skip a class.

I'm just too happy to pay attention right now. And to think, I woke up this morning thinking things couldn't get any better.

All I can think is that I want to tell Jani, but she's at work, and my shift starts in a little while as well. I'll just bring her some food when I go on my lunch break. And maybe flowers. Do guys still give flowers or is that lame? I've never given a woman flowers, but I've never really been in a relationship before. There's no way I'm asking the guys. I'll never hear the end of it.

Cassidy sits on Samantha's step when I turn onto Violent Circle. Cass moved not too long ago, but she comes back to visit. You can take the girl out of the circle, but not the circle out of the girl.

She waves when I park and make my way over to her. "Hey, Cass. I hear you're launching your own business."

She smiles, tugging one of her socks up. "Sort of. I'm just selling my animals online. I spend most of my time at the community center. I hear you found a girlfriend." Cass has rooted for me from the beginning with Jani.

"Yeah." I take a seat beside her on the step. "I need some advice. I'm going to pop in on Jani at work to bring her lunch later and I was wondering…is it totally lame to bring flowers?"

I'm instantly sorry since both women look at me like I'm a puppy who tripped over his ears.

"That's so sweet!" Samantha says.

Cass beams at me. "Definitely not lame. She'll love it. Lilies are her favorite."

I need to get out of here before they start patting me on the head. "Thanks, I'd better get moving."

They both stare at me with that *aww* expression as I rush to my car.

A smile is plastered across my face as I stroll through the supercenter, stopping to chat with other employees. One of the few things—other than preventing me from starving—that this job has been good for is meeting new people. From teenagers working their first job corralling carts in the parking lot, to a few cashiers that have to be pushing eighty, I've met so many interesting people from all walks of life. There is a camaraderie because we all have one thing in common—we hate our jobs and can't wait to get the hell out.

Today I get to put in my notice. I've decided to put in the minimum two weeks, so I'll have a week off before starting my new job. It's been a long four years. I've earned a little break. Besides, most just quit by not showing up.

I'm approached by Ty, one of the general managers. "Noble! I'm short a man in the parking lot today, and your department is overstaffed for this shift. I'm going to move you for today." He hands me a two-way radio.

Any other day, I'd be cursing his name. We're in full blown holiday mode now, and working the lot means loading TV's, trampolines, and a hundred other large items into customer's cars while they bitch about how you're doing it. You wouldn't believe how many show up in a tiny car and I'm somehow supposed to magically fit a massive item inside. Oh sure, I can shove a whole swimming pool into your Ford Focus, buddy, no problem. All the while trying not to get run over because in our bright yellow vests, we're somehow invisible.

But nothing can kill my mood today. I have a scholarship, a new job, and the girl I've been after forever. Life is good.

"I got it." I clip the radio on my belt. "I'm headed back to put in my notice, though. This is my last two weeks."

Ty stares at me. "Did something happen? I know you aren't on great terms with your department manager, but…"

"It's not Kori. I mean, she's terrible, but the whole store knows that. I can handle her. I got an internship at WFUK. They want me to start after the holidays."

Ty sticks his hand out. "Congratulations. I'm sorry to lose you. You have an excellent work ethic, young man."

"Thank you."

The radio crackles to life and Josh's voice blares through the speaker. "I need some help out here!"

Josh has always and probably will always work the lot. He's a die-hard stoner with half a brain, and one of the few people I don't like working with. He's lazy, and spends most of the time following me around talking about bullshit while I work. Cart pushers are hard to keep because the job is more difficult than it looks. Stacked together, the carts are heavy, and you're at the mercy of the weather. That, and the fact that his uncle works in corporate, are the only reasons he's made it this far without being fired.

"I'd better get moving." Ty nods at me. "I'm covering Tire and Lube today, so just hit me on the radio if you get backed up."

"Will do." I make a quick trip to the human resources office in the rear of the store. Giving my notice doesn't actually require me to tell the managers in person, since I just have to enter it into the computer, but I still can't wait until Kori finds out. Because of her reputation, the meat department has become notoriously hard to staff, and with me leaving in the middle of the Christmas rush, I'm screwing her, royally. Like I said, life is good.

I don't bother to stop by my department to tell her I've been moved to the parking lot for the day either. She'll figure it out. In the beginning, I didn't have such a negative attitude toward this job. It wasn't until she took over with her gossipy, mean girl attitude, that I started to hate it.

I've worked here for almost four years, and during that time have missed a total of two days of work. One because of a schedule mix up where they had me scheduled for the same day as my final exams, and another when I was sick and puking every five minutes.

When I came back in the next day, still sick and feverish, but well enough to soldier through it, the other employees all gave me looks like I was headed to a guillotine. Then I started getting warnings from them. *Kori was so pissed you called out yesterday. There was a truck and she had to do it. You're in so much trouble. She said she's going to write you up.* And I don't mean a couple people mentioned it. Almost everyone I passed had some dire warning for me. The damn soda delivery guy who spends three hours a week here knew I called out and she was pissed. She spent the whole day bad mouthing me.

Up until that point, I had always tried to be a team player, came in on days off when they needed me, did jobs she asked me to do that were not my responsibility, like inventory. After that?

Fuck no. I do my job, get my check, and get the hell out. Judging by the way the other managers respect me though, it must still be better than the effort they get from other employees.

It's chilly out, so I grab a coffee and stop by my car for my heavier coat before grabbing the cart mule and getting to work. For someone who was so behind that he had to call for help over the radio, Josh is nowhere to be seen. After a quick glance around to make sure no one is watching, I pop in a wireless earbud and choose a playlist on my phone. Time to get to work.

It takes me almost an hour to clear the entire lot, and I'm just taking a breather, scanning the lot for any I may have missed, when Kori storms up to me. A sudden idea pops into my head, and I flip the talk switch on the radio. I'm done taking her shit. Every manager carries a radio and a lot of employees do as well. Whatever she's about to say is going to get broadcast across the highest levels of the store.

"Noble! Are you fucking retarded? There are four pallets sitting in the back that need stocked."

Silence. I pretend I didn't even hear her until she grabs my arm. "Are you deaf?"

"No, I'm not deaf. And take your hand off of me right now." I stare her in the eye and clearly enunciate the words. "Do not touch me."

Perplexed, she lets go but continues her tirade. "Get inside and stock the fresh wall."

"Ty put me out here for the day. If you have a problem with that, I suggest you take it up with him."

Her face reddens. "You work in my department! I don't give a shit what that flaming queer has to say."

Oh. Oh this is so good. Yeah, Ty is gay, and his boyfriend works here as well, in electronics. They are well liked by everyone, except this bitch. And everyone just heard that.

I just need to push her a little further. "Oh, by the way, Kori, I just put in my notice. So you'll need to adjust the schedule for the end of the month."

Until this moment, I was unaware a human face could turn purple. I'm waiting on steam to shoot out of her ears because she kind of looks like a cartoon right now. Her hands are planted on her hips, her face screwed up like she tasted something bad.

"It's less than a month until Christmas! You can't leave me short-handed like that!"

Leaning against the outer brick wall of the Tire and Lube section, I cross my arms. "I'm moving on to bigger and better things. You'll just have to train someone else to do inventory for you, plus all the other little jobs that are supposed to be your responsibility. I wonder what management would think if they knew you gave me the inventory codes. I mean, I'm just a lowly employee after all."

She steps toward me with a sneer. "You think anyone would believe you? Please, I get what I want in this place, haven't you figured that out by now?"

"Sure, but I'm not willing to suck an assortment of dicks just to get an extra dollar an hour and a manager pin on my vest."

Sputtering, she can't seem to get any words out. Finally, she shrieks the words, "You're fired, you worthless little shit!"

Smiling, I bounce off of the wall. "Sure, as soon as I hear that from Ty, Jimmy, or Niall—the only managers who can actually fire an employee—I'll be gone before you can say karma."

She doesn't get a chance to reply because the sudden *ahem* from behind her draws her attention. Ty, Jimmy, and—holy shit—the big district manager stand behind her, radios in hand.

"Ty," I say amiably, nodding at him.

"Carts are piling up. Better get back to work," he says to me, his hardened gaze never leaving Kori's face. "And check your radio. You left the channel open."

All the blood drains from Kori's face as I reach down to flip the switch. "Did I? Sorry about that. It's been a big week, finding out about my scholarship, new job and all. In my excitement, I must've forgotten to turn it off."

I'm not trying to fool anyone, and he knows it. The ear to ear grin on my face is a dead giveaway. He swallows back his own grin, shakes his head, and gestures to the cart mule.

"I'm on it!" I chirp.

God, what I'd give to hear the conversation going on

behind me now. They not only heard the way she talks to employees, but the fact that she had me doing her managerial duties I wasn't trained for. Plus, she used a gay slur against Ty and called me retarded.

Awesome.

Josh finally catches up with me as I'm hooking carts to the mule. The mule is a machine that helps push the carts inside, sparing our backs the extra weight. It takes a little practice to learn to steer it, but by the end of my first day, I had it down.

"Dude, do you know the whole store heard you tell her she sucked her way to the top?" Josh asks, lighting a cigarette. "I was talking to that Ginny chick on register four and all the cashiers heard it. Some customers too."

"Uh-huh. The other mule is charged, Josh, if you want to start working the other side of the lot."

"Oh? No one told you? I'm not allowed to use the mule anymore. I hit another car."

Yeah, he said *another*. I believe this makes three.

"It was a sharp ass Mustang, brand new, still had the paper tag in the back window. Mule scraped all the way down the side." He angles his hand and makes a high-pitched screeching noise. There isn't a hint of remorse or embarrassment in his voice. "So I have to get them by hand now. I got suspended for a day too, because I ran."

He what? Pausing, I turn back to him. "You ran? After you hit the car? Ran where?"

"Yeah, the dude saw me, and he was coming toward me, looking all pissed. So I took off. I didn't really think about where I was going, just, you know, away." He gestures to the field beside us that separates the supercenter from a warehouse.

A snort of laughter jumps out of me as I picture it. It's not hard to imagine Josh hitting a car and just running for it, but I imagine the car owner had to think he was beyond stupid. We're surrounded by cameras. "Tends to happen when you damage someone's ride."

"Fuck off. I panicked. Anyway, I got suspended a day. Today's my first day back."

I back the mule out and angle it toward the cart return doors. Josh follows along, babbling about random stuff while I work. "Dude, look at that car." He points out an Impala, dropped so low, it's nearly dragging the ground. Letters stenciled across the bottom of the doors read, *Too Low for a Fat Ho*.

"Classy," I remark. It's far from the most ridiculous thing I've seen out here.

A few minutes later, Kori bursts through the doors and gives me the blackest look of hate I've ever been thrown. I'm waiting for her head to spin around or green, pea colored puke to start flying. Without a word, she stalks to her car.

Wow. Her shift is far from over. I wonder if he fired her. I don't have to wonder long before Ty calls my name over the radio and asks me to meet him in the human resources office.

"Great," Josh whines. "I have to do this all myself."

Ty and Jimmy are sitting in the office when I come in. I take a seat and grin at them. "You wanted to see me, boss?" I glance from one to the other, almost giddy. "Bosses," I correct.

I can't help it. I've eaten so much shit over the past four years because I needed this job. These guys have been okay, but they're responsible for promoting Kori to get rid of her instead of firing her. Maybe she's related to a big shot too. Nepotism runs rampant around here.

"Kori gave you the inventory code? You were doing the orders?"

Sitting back. I shrug. "Sometimes it was me, sometimes it was her. I did it when she asked me to."

"That's all we needed to know," Ty says, and turns to Jimmy. "That will justify the suspension."

Jimmy nods, gets to his feet, and heads for the door. "I'll go put it in."

Once he's gone, Ty turns to me. "Noble, I like you."

"But I'm fired," I interrupt. It isn't hard to guess where he was going. Regret drips from his face.

Ty grins, rubbing his chin. "Let's just say I accepted your resignation and it's unnecessary for you to work out the two weeks notice."

"It was the dick sucking, wasn't it?"

Ty bursts out laughing. "Half the damn store heard that."

"Yeah, sorry, I thought they already knew."

We're both laughing when Jimmy returns, eyeing me. "Everything okay?"

I get to my feet. "Yeah, we're good. I have four weeks paid vacation piled up. Will you make sure Harriet doesn't forget to add that to my last check?"

"I'll do that."

The final click of my nametag when I take it off is a welcome sound. I hand it and the vest to Jimmy. "So, Kori's suspended?"

Ty sighs, and I actually feel a little sorry for him. Even at the top, this job sucks. "For now. And on probation when she returns."

"Are we kicking zombie ass tonight?" Jimmy asks.

"Yep. I got some free time," I chuckle. "See you, guys, I'm going to get the hell out of here."

I have to grab a few things I keep stashed in my cubby in the meat department on my way out. I'm about to push open the employee only doors when a voice calls from behind me.

I know that voice.

I don't know her name, but this woman is the most annoying customer ever. At least once a week she appears like the wicked witch of the west. I swear, I look around for a puff of red smoke whenever I see her. Generally, she comes to argue with me over prices—something I have no control over—or to return some rotten meat she bought weeks ago and swears went bad instantly. She's a pain in the ass.

"Excuse me!" She gestures to the bunker full of frozen turkeys. "Do these turkeys get any bigger?"

"No, ma'am. They're dead," I reply cheerfully.

Some people can't take a joke.

A scowl breaks across her face. "I know that! Do you have any over twenty pounds?"

If we do, I'm sure they're still buried on the pallet and this isn't my responsibility anymore. If she wasn't a bitch, I would've called another employee to help her, but I'm done catering to people like this. "No, sorry. That's all we have."

Her hands clamp onto her hips and she bends over slightly. Between her stance and the way her skinny face seems to come to a point, she looks like a chicken. "You just don't want to bother looking! I insist you go in the back and bring me a twenty pound turkey! Or I'll speak to your manager about your rudeness!"

Forcing a smile onto my face, I nod. "Sure thing, ma'am. Just wait right here. It may take a few minutes."

Satisfied she has gotten her way, she nods smugly, and I head through the doors. This is a common thing with customers that drives all retail employees nuts. They seem to think the storeroom is piled high with products that we just don't want to put on the shelves. Most of the time, if you can't see it, we don't have it. When we know we're out of something, but they insist I check, I generally just go back and play on my phone for a few minutes then come out and tell them again, that we're out.

The sound of gagging draws my attention and I can't help but laugh at the sight of Ricky, one of the other meat department employees, running over to the trash can. He stands over it for a minute until the urge to puke passes, not even noticing I'm there.

I'm not laughing because he's sick, it's the reason why. Packages of expired chicken, pork, beef, and—horror of horrors— fish are stacked on the counter, awaiting disposal. It occurs to me I'll never get stuck with that job again, and nothing could tear the smile from my face.

"Ricky, are you okay?"

"Yeah, that shrimp one got me, plus Fester is almost full."

Fester is what we named the large barrel that we dump all the spoiled meat into. It isn't too bad when the meat stays refrigerated until it's tossed, but Kori gets a sick pleasure from setting all the meat out for hours, sometimes overnight, before ordering someone to slice open the packages and deposit it in the bucket. Fester only gets picked up every seven to ten days, so just opening it is enough to make anyone puke.

Ricky composes himself and grins at me. "I heard you on the radio. Did they fire her?"

"Of course not. She's suspended though." I gesture to the rotting meat pile. "It'd be a good time to talk to Ty about shit like this."

"Maybe I will." He shakes his head. "Do you want to help?"

"Sorry, I'm off the clock. For good, actually."

Ricky blinks, taking a step back. "Shit, man, they fired you? Was it the dick remark?"

"I had just put in my notice, and they told me there's no need to finish the two weeks. I've got another job."

"Lucky son of a bitch."

Yeah, I really am. "Yep. It was good working with you, Ricky. I'll see you around."

"See you." With a grim expression, he turns and picks up a rotted beef roast, and I get the hell out before the smell can reach me.

I grab my stuff, and cut through the dairy department's storeroom. I come out near the front doors and smile to myself as I make my way through them for the first time as a former employee. I wonder how long that obnoxious customer will stand back there before she realizes I'm not coming back? Poor Ricky is probably going to get stuck with her.

I'm going to see my girl, take her some flowers, and tell her about the internship.

After I buy the flowers, and stop at the diner to pick up our lunch, I get to Scarlet Toys just as Clarence, another of the employees is walking in.

"Are those for me?" he teases, nodding to the flowers.

"And risk having your boyfriend beat the crap out of me? Not likely."

Laughing, he accompanies me inside. Jani sits on the floor surrounded by a bunch of black straps and a sheet of printed instructions.

"Are you busy?" I ask, and I'm thrilled to see the smile that jumps onto her face.

"I'm trying to put together this sex swing contraption, but I'm afraid I might hang myself. What are you doing here?"

"I brought you lunch."

"And lilies?" she says, grinning and getting to her feet.

"No, these are for me. They really bring out my eyes, don't you think?" I bat my eyelashes at her as she slings her arms around my neck.

"They're white. Your eyes are blue."

"It makes perfect sense if you don't think about it."

"Oh, like our relationship." She drops a kiss on my lips.

Little smart ass.

I squeeze her ass with one hand and murmur in her ear. "Do I need to take you home and remind you why we make sense?"

Her eyes betray just how much she'd love for me to do that. "Later," she whispers. A smile stretches across her face as she takes the flowers and sniffs them. "Thank you. I love lilies."

"Can you take a break?"

"Sure." She leads me to their break room and peeks into the bag of food I've brought. "Mmm, curly fries always smell so good."

Laughing, I unpack the food and we sit down to eat. "You mean fries smell good," I tease her. "It doesn't matter if they're curly."

Her mouth drops open. "You have to be kidding! Curly fries smell way better!" She grabs a curly fry from the carton and pops it into her mouth.

"You're delusional. They're just cut different."

"Fine. We'll prove it." She gets to her feet and grabs a blindfold. We might be in one of the few places in the world where you can just reach out and find a blindfold.

She slips it over her eyes. "Hold a curly fry or a regular one under my nose and I'll tell you which it is."

She giggles when I hold a regular French fry under her nose. "Regular fry, easy."

I switch to another fry from the same bag, and she shakes her head. "Nice try, it's still a regular fry."

Damn, she really can tell. As soon as I try the curly fry, she knows. "That's a curly one. See, they smell better!" Her giggles fill the room, and I can't wipe the smile from my face. Damn, I'm crazy about this girl.

"Fine, I was wrong." I pull the blindfold off of her. "You can tell the difference."

Beaming, she says, "Oh, I'm going to need to hear that again."

"You can tell the difference," I chuckle, taking a bite of my burger.

"No, the first part." I want to kiss the impish grin off of her face as she sips her soda.

"You were right."

Her eyes close and she hums. "Mmm, one more time."

"Not the most humble winner are you?"

Her eyes pop open. "Please, I'm the most modest person you'll ever meet."

"Clearly. So, I have some news. How would you feel about dating a guy who just quit his job?"

Her eyebrows shoot up. "You quit the supercenter? What happened?"

"I may have announced over the radio that my manager sucked dick to get where she was."

Jani bursts out laughing. "Oh my god. The bitchy one who always tortures you?"

"Yep." I take a drink and wait for her response.

"That must've felt good. Tell me what happened."

Tilting my head, I gaze at her for a moment. "You aren't worried about dating a deadbeat without a job?"

"Please," she scoffs. "I know you, and you always work. You're no deadbeat. And there's only so much shit anyone is willing to take. I got fired for answering the phone with *Hello caller, you're on the air* at the burger place so I'm not one to judge."

"Well." I swallow my last bite and sit back in my seat. "You'll be happy to know I'm not actually unemployed. I got offered an internship at WFUK starting after the holidays. I put in my two weeks notice, but I didn't last long since I couldn't give a shit anymore."

She grabs my arm and squeezes, shaking it back and forth a little. "You got a job at the station? That's wonderful!"

"I'll probably be fetching coffee and sweeping floors, but it beats the hell out of the supercenter. Higher wage, and I get college credit. I don't know what kind of hours I'll have yet, though."

"We should celebrate." She leans across the table. "Hypothetically, if I were to show up at your place tonight with movies and pizza, wearing my tiniest pair of panties, how would you react?"

"The panties are completely unnecessary. I'll have them off of you before the pizza is cold."

"Noted."

I'm a lucky son of a bitch.

Chapter Six

January

The past few weeks with Noble have flown by. He's been busy studying for final exams, so he doesn't have a whole lot of time, but he goes out of his way to spend as much of it with me as he can. He's the first guy to really make me a priority, and I'd be lying if I said it doesn't make me feel good and completely terrify me at the same time.

Yeah, I have more issues than Playboy magazine, and I'm trying not to let my irrational fear of living my mother's life mess up my own.

"Jani," Mom calls from the living room.

I run my brush through my hair one more time before joining her. "Are you feeling okay?" I ask, taking a seat on the couch. I'm sure it's annoying, but that's usually my first question for her.

"Fine, honey." She fumbles with her phone and sets it aside. "I was just talking to Leon, and he invited us for Christmas."

"Pass," I mumble. Leon is mom's older brother. He's filthy rich and never lets anyone forget it. Don't get me wrong, I don't have a problem with rich people. Take Cassidy's fiancé Wyatt, for example. He could buy and sell Leon, but he's an honest, good hearted man who would never flaunt it. Leon is a pretentious dick who loves to show off how much "better" he is.

Mom gives me the look. You know what I'm talking about. It's the same look all mothers seem to give when they're fed up with you. "I know you don't like him, but it might be good to get away for a bit." Her grin widens. "It's two weeks in Hawaii, January, and you could bring Noble."

The fact that even the thought of spending two weeks on a beach with a half-naked Noble isn't enough to make me want to go shows how much I actively dislike this man.

"You should go, Mom, if you want to."

"Leon said he'd pay for the plane tickets, and we can stay with them. Are you sure you don't want to go?"

"I'm sure, but you should go. I know you haven't seen him or aunt Helen in a long time. Do you feel like you can handle the plane ride and everything?"

Mom laughs and rolls her eyes. "For the chance to lie on the beach for two weeks? I'll manage. I don't want to leave you alone on Christmas, though."

"Cass and Wyatt invited me over for Christmas dinner," I lie. "I'll be fine." I don't want her to miss out on something she wants to do just because of me. I'm really not bothered about Christmas. I'll keep Scarlet Toys open and just work if Wyatt wants me to. They probably would've invited me, but they're going away for their own little holiday.

"Well, if you're sure…"

"Call and have him book your flight. Then call in your prescriptions and I'll pick them up. You don't want to run out while you're there."

"What would I do without you?" she asks, picking up her phone.

By the next morning, everything is set, and I drop her off at the airport to catch her incredibly expensive last minute flight to Hawaii. "Don't forget to call me when you land!" I call out as she walks away.

"I will! You make sure you take advantage of having an empty apartment! I want grandbabies, you know!"

The crowd of people between us erupt in laughter, and I

shake my head. Isn't that a parent's job in life? To embarrass their kids? She's a natural.

I am looking forward to two whole weeks by myself though.

I have just enough time to get ready and get to work after I drop her off. I have to go in early because I planned something a little different for Christmas at Scarlet Toys. Cass and Wyatt have arranged a holiday party at the community center, complete with a Santa to take pictures with the kids, and it made me think, why not a Santa at Scarlet?

Henry, the new guy I hired to take my old position since I became the manager, didn't blink an eye when I explained what we were going to do, so that's a good sign he'll work out.

Henry and Martha have been decorating with the traditional stuff like snowflakes and candy canes, and the place looks great. Martha helps customers while I clear out a large space in the corner, set up a tree, and cover a large chair with a swatch of red felt. My decorations won't be as tame.

Henry keeps throwing glances my way and laughing as I proceed to trim the tree with tiny penis shaped lights and various sex toys as ornaments. He seems particularly amused by the large fleshlight I use as the tree topper.

"What? It's red and white. That's festive!" I insist.

"And the blow up doll just screams Christmas," he laughs.

I grab a headband with reindeer antlers attached and put them on the doll. "There. Problem solved."

"Woo-hoo, well, knock me down and steal my teeth, what have we got here?"

Henry is too busy fighting back laughter at Martha and her country exclamations to reply as I make my way to the front of the store where two strippers have just walked in.

The guy is decked out in a Santa suit, minus the fake white beard, since he has a very real beard that is too damn sexy. His Santa suit is far from traditional. I don't think I've ever seen a Santa in bright red spandex shorts, connected to white suspenders that stretch over his bare, well- built chest. His shiny black boots complete the outfit.

The woman is wearing a little more, but her skin tight red bodysuit leaves nothing to the imagination, and those black garters are going to be a big hit, even if her stockings do end at a goofy pair of elf shoes.

"Hi, I'm St. Dick, and this is Gumdrop. Where do you want us?"

I'm tempted by the plethora of inappropriate responses I could give him, but I control it. "Right over here. You'll just be playing Santa and taking pictures with the customers."

"Sounds good."

It's a big hit. I swear this town is way more dirty minded than they like to pretend. People line up all day to sit on their laps and have their pictures taken. Stripper Santa is posing for his last picture with two giggling college girls when Noble walks in.

The smile that washes over his face at the sight of the stripper elf fades when it lands on the two girls posing with Santa.

"Hey." I give him a quick hug. "Sorry, I forgot you were picking me up tonight."

"Hey, Noble!" one of the girls calls out. "Come and get a picture with us! We're going to flash the camera!"

Oh hell no. How do they know him anyway? It's not like he knows every girl at the college. It takes every ounce of my self-control to reign in the jealousy at the thought of two trollops hanging on my guy, but I manage. I want to see his response.

Shaking his head, he totally ignores them. "Can you get out of here soon?"

"Sure, let me talk to Clarence for a sec." To his credit, he seems to have no interest in the two women vying for his attention, even when they both yank their shirts up for a picture. They wear identical expressions of disappointment when he looks away from them.

Ha ha, that's right, bitches. Mine.

I have a quick word with Clarence about closing up, grab my stuff, and join Noble, who is now lingering by the door like he can't wait to leave.

"How do you know the titty sisters in there?" I ask, following him to his car.

"From school," he replies. It strikes me as a little odd he doesn't elaborate, but I don't push it. After all, he didn't want any part of them, so I'm not worried.

We head back to my now empty apartment and sprawl out on the couch. "So, your mom is gone until after New Year's?" Noble asks.

"Yeah, she's visiting her brother."

A bright smile inches across his face. "So, you could go with me then. I wasn't going to ask because I knew you wouldn't want to leave your mom alone."

Noble has holiday plans to visit his mother in Ohio for a couple of days, then his father in northern Indiana. "I'm not going to intrude on your family visit."

His expression hardens. "You aren't intruding. I want to introduce you to my parents. Just be warned, they're a little weird."

"All parents are," I laugh. My teeth rake across my lip as I consider it. I'm flattered and excited he wants me to meet his parents. I'm also curious and nosy as hell so this will give me a chance to learn more about him and how he grew up. "Are you sure?"

"Absolutely. Can you leave Scarlet Toys for a week?"

I think on it for a moment. "I already planned to close Christmas Eve and Christmas Day. I should be able to juggle the schedule and take a week off, if it's okay with Wyatt."

"Good." He slaps me on the ass. "Now, where's my dinner?"

"Between my legs."

His lips curl up. "Good. I'm starving."

Wyatt is cool with me delegating some responsibilities to Clarence for a week, so I'm all set to meet Noble's parents. I'm also practically rattling with anxiety. I've never been in a serious relationship, and this one has taken a leap forward into that territory pretty quickly. I don't usually care what anyone thinks of me, but I want his family to like me.

Noble grins down at me as we stand on his mother's porch. "Aw, the fearless January is nervous."

"Shut up," I hiss, as he unlocks the front door.

"It's adorable."

I want to ask him how adorable I'll be when I pop out his eyes and stick them down his pants so he can watch me kick his ass, but the words catch in my throat as the door is thrown open and a petite blonde almost knocks him over.

"Damn, Ma, did you miss me?" Noble chuckles, hugging her and half carrying her back inside.

"Maybe if you'd call me once in a while, Noble Bradley!"

She turns to me with a soft smile. "You must be January. I'm Michelle. Come in, and tell me all about yourself."

Noble takes my coat and disappears while I'm led into a cozy living room decorated in soft shades of blue. I take a seat on the couch, and she sits across from me. Before we can talk, Noble pokes his head around the corner.

"Ma, you want a drink?"

"No thanks." She turns to me. "So, you're the neighbor Noble has talked about forever. You're beautiful. No wonder he's so smitten. It's good to finally meet you. My boy had better be treating you right."

Noble enters with two sodas in hand, just in time to hear her.

"He's good to me," I assure her, grinning at Noble.

"Of course I am. And she's crazy about me. All her friends tell me so. All she can talk about is Noble, Noble, Noble."

Michelle laughs and shakes her head as I elbow him. "It's a little early to shovel bullshit, Goose."

Oh, there's no way I'm letting that nickname pass, especially when I see his expression the second the word leaves her mouth.

"Goose?" I repeat, raising my eyebrow.

"Oh yes, I've called him that since he was two. Couldn't keep his hands to himself, this one. Always grabbing someone's bottom. I can't count the times I got called to his preschool."

Some things never change. Bumping my shoulder against Noble's, I ask. "When did he finally stop?"

"A little girl in Kindergarten popped him right in the nose for it, and he finally learned his lesson."

Giggles spill out of me. "That is the best thing I've ever heard."

"Of course, then he had a crush on the little girl, so it was an ongoing issue." Noble's cheeks flush.

"Always the ladies man, huh?" See, this is some of the dirt I was hoping for. He teases me all the time. It's good to have some ammunition.

"What can I say? This face is a burden sometimes."

His mother and I both scoff, and he throws his arm around me. "Ma, tell me about the new guy you're seeing."

It's his mother's turn to blush a little. "Bruce is a math teacher at the high school. You may remember him—"

"Mr. Dendron?" Noble interrupts. "You're dating Mr. Dendron? The guy with the dent in his forehead?"

"Noble! Yes, that's him."

Turning to me, he says, "Kids called him Mr. Dent because he has a hollow spot on one side of his forehead. It was deep. Like, lay him on his back and you could've poured a cup of water into it."

"Poor guy. What happened?"

Michelle speaks up. "It was from a car accident when he was a kid. He has a metal plate in his skull and it caused the indention." She gives Noble a look. "He's a very nice guy."

Noble holds up his hands. "I wasn't saying anything. I'm just surprised. Mr. Dent—Dendron was always nice to me. I aced his class."

"He's helping me since I got roped into teaching a four-week long sex education class. He teaches the boys part of the time." Her gaze falls on me, and the corner of her mouth tucks in. "You can imagine how middle school boys react to sex education."

Noble chuckles. "I remember stealing the pads they handed out to the girls and sticking them to lockers. One guy took a pad to lunch, stuck it to a table, then dripped a whole can of soda onto it to see how much it could hold."

With Noble's sense of humor, good looks, and easygoing personality, I can easily picture him as the popular boy in school.

We sit and chat for over an hour. Noble's mom is sweet, funny, and clearly not above embarrassing him for fun. I like her instantly.

Michelle sighs and turns to me. "You'll have to excuse me tonight because I have an early day tomorrow. It's the last day of classes, but the sex ed one is bright and early."

"Of course."

"I made a lasagna for dinner if you two haven't eaten. It's warming in the oven," she says to Noble, getting to her feet. She kisses him on the forehead. "We'll all go out to dinner tomorrow night."

"Sounds good, Ma."

"So, what would you like to do, Goose?" I ask, after she heads upstairs.

His lips twitch as he tries not to laugh. "That name never leaves this house."

"Aw, I think it's cute." I pat his chest.

He reaches over and pinches my ass, making me yelp. "Every time you say goose, you get goosed, fair warning. Do you want to see my room?"

"Do you have cartoon character sheets?"

Chuckling, he takes my hand and pulls me to my feet. "Nope, but I'll get some if that's what you're into."

Noble's bedroom is huge. It's two rooms, actually, in the renovated attic. A queen-sized bed sits against a wall, wrapped in freshly laundered sheets. A large television hangs on the far wall, angled so it can be seen from the bed.

The next room has an oversized recliner, table, and what I assume is another television. "Two TV's? Spoiled much?" I tease.

"It's a monitor." He gestures to the shelf beneath it where three game systems sit side by side. "For the games. And yes, but I spoiled myself. I worked summers for this setup."

Turning to face him, I slide my arms around his waist. "I

like it."

He plants a soft kiss on my lips, and I laugh when his stomach lets out a loud growl. "Hungry?"

"Starved. Do you want some lasagna? Then we could watch a movie downstairs, if you aren't tired."

"Sounds good to me."

Noble dishes up the lasagna, and I swear he wolfs it down in about three seconds. I can never understand how guys do that without choking to death. We talk while I finish my food, and I try to keep my voice down so I won't wake his mother. It's sort of ingrained in me after having my mom live with me. Noble pops our dishes into the dishwasher before we move to the living room.

We find a movie and curl up together on the couch. Noble grabs a throw blanket and wraps it around us. He murmurs in my ear. "You're smiling."

"It's snowing." His gaze follows mine to the window where snow falls softly, and we watch in silence for a few moments, wrapped around one another. I'm warm, full, and utterly content.

His hands slowly wander over my body under the blanket, and he presses a warm kiss just under my ear. "I love your neck. It's long and pretty." Another brush of his lips against my neck sends a shiver through me. "And so soft."

My eyes fall closed, and I tilt my head, encouraging him to keep going. I slip my hands under his shirt to trace the muscles of his abdomen, reveling in the feel of his heated skin. God, this guy can get me hot in about two seconds.

As if he's reading my mind, he whispers, "I love how quickly you respond to me. I'll bet you're wet already aren't you?"

"I can't help it. You turn me on. I love your stomach, and these." I trace his pelvic V lines with a fingertip. "They might be my favorite."

A wicked smile tilts his lips. "If that's your favorite part of me, I have work to do tonight."

He pulls me onto his lap, my back against his chest, my legs resting on either side of his. He spreads his legs which pulls mine apart, and I lean back against him as his hand slides down the front of my pants and under my panties.

"Your mother," I whisper.

"Is three rooms away and sleeps like the dead," he assures me, adjusting the blanket over our laps.

He rubs his fingers between my legs with just the right amount of pressure, and I couldn't give a twirly fuck about getting caught anymore. It feels so good. I don't know how long we stay that way, his fingers slowly working me up while fluttery kisses land on my neck and shoulders. My body takes over, grinding against his hard cock beneath me as I draw closer and closer.

His fingers stop moving, and he murmurs in my ear. "Do you feel that? That urge driving you crazy? Making you squirm and press your legs together? That's how I feel every fucking time I see you, January. It's torture. Incredible, sexy as fuck torture."

"Don't stop," I plead.

He resumes, his fingers moving faster. "I'm going to make you come right here. Then I'm taking you up to my room and bending you over my bed."

His words are enough to send me hurtling toward the sky, and I turn my head to sink my teeth into the fleshy skin where his neck meets his shoulder as I fight to stay quiet through a devastating orgasm. I've just met his mother, and heavy sleeper or not, I'm not taking the chance of being remembered as the girl who came on her couch.

Before I can recover, he scoops me up and carries me upstairs. I love how strong he is, the way he can grab me up like it's nothing. His door barely has time to close behind us and he has my pants around my ankles, bending me over the arm of his recliner.

I've never actually done it this way before and it's incredibly hot. Especially because we don't undress or anything. He just yanks his pants down, slides on a condom, and plunges into me like he can't bear to wait another second.

My hands fist the soft material of the chair as he pounds into me like a man possessed. "Noble, yes, fuck." Nonsense spills out of my lips as I'm fucked harder than I've ever been. Noble isn't small, and there's a little pain because he's so deep, but I don't care. It's nothing compared to the pleasure streaking through every inch of me.

It's never been like this with anyone. So rough and dirty and primal. It isn't until I hear a chuckle that I open my eyes and realize the lights are flashing on and off at a weird, but steady pace. What the hell? Is there a problem with the electricity?

Noble's fingers trail between my cheeks and over the place that no one has ever touched, and the lights are forgotten as I stiffen up a little. "Relax, beautiful," he murmurs, pushing my shirt up to my neck. He runs his other hand lightly down my spine. "If you don't like it, just tell me to stop."

I feel the rush of heat sweep across my sweaty face as he rubs his finger on the tight little hole, sending a sensation through me I've never felt before. Embarrassment wars with lust, but I lose all sense of rational thought when he slips his finger in.

His pace has slowed, but his cock is hitting my spot just right and with the added sensation of his finger in a forbidden area, I'm gone. I'm not even aware that he's removed his finger until I feel his hands clamped on my hips as he slams into me a few times before releasing a long groan.

His sweaty chest sticks to my back as he bends over me, dropping little kisses down my back. "Are you okay?"

"As long as I don't have to walk anywhere for a few days, I'm peachy."

Laughing, he steps back and helps me stand on my wobbly legs. We're standing there with our pants and underwear around our ankles, just looking into each other's eyes, but it doesn't feel weird. "Was I too rough?" he asks.

"No." I run my lips over his jaw, and kiss the corner of his mouth. "I loved it."

Smiling, he kicks off his pants and underwear, then kneels to remove mine. "I want to sleep naked with you."

Between not trusting his roommates not to barge in, and having my mom a room away, we never get to do that. I take his shirt off him and he does the same for me. We each take a turn in his bathroom to clean up a little before we climb into bed.

Remembering the weird flickering, I ask, "What was up

with the lights?"

Laughing, he pulls me closer to him until I lay my head on his chest. Then he claps his hands and the lights go out.

What the—

"You have a clapper?" I didn't even know they still made those.

"Had it since I was a kid. The light switch is all the way across the room. I didn't want to have to get out of bed. I've never actually fucked in this room, though."

The realization hits me, and I burst out laughing. "The noise...the slapping of your balls against me was turning the lights on and off."

"Or my cock is so amazing it disrupted the electrical field and sent out an EMP to screw up the lights."

"And you're supposed to be a scientist," I giggle. "I'm telling Cass about this, just so you know. This might be worse than her Scooby story."

"Scooby story?"

Giggling, I snuggle into him. "Ask her next time you see her."

His arms tighten around me as I drift off to sleep.

The smell of bacon and coffee wakes me the next morning, and I groan at the ache that has settled into my muscles. I need to get more exercise if I'm going to keep up with Noble. I pull on Noble's shirt and my panties, grab my clean clothes, and head to the shower.

The hot water feels amazing, loosening up my muscles and making me feel halfway human again. There's no help for my vagina though. It feels like it went a couple of rounds with a heavyweight boxer.

I'm lathering up my hair, letting the hot water beat against my back when the shower curtain is abruptly yanked open. Okay, if I had taken a second to think about it, I would have realized that it was Noble standing there. I mean, who else would it be? But you don't sneak up on a girl when she's vulnerable, and standing naked with a head full of soap definitely qualifies. Still, screeching and slinging the palm full of shampoo at him may have been an overreaction.

"Shit!" He steps back and clamps his hands over his eyes. "Sorry! You scared the hell out of me."

"So you throw acid in my face?"

"It's shampoo." I grab a washcloth, wet it, and try to help by wiping at his eyes.

Apparently, he doesn't trust me because he takes a step back, trips over my clothes on the floor, and bangs his knee against the sink which knocks his phone right into the toilet.

Feeling around, he manages to turn the sink faucet on and rinse his eyes. They're red and watering when he looks at me, and I squeak, "Sorry." His gaze moves to the toilet where his phone is currently drowning. "Is it waterproof?"

"Yeah."

He continues to stand there staring at the toilet like it might spit the phone out on its own while I rinse my hair.

"Noble?"

"Um-Hmm."

"Are you going to get your phone? It's not pee water if that's what you're worried about."

With a sigh, he sits on the edge of the tub. "I'm not going be able to do it."

"What? Why? Just grab it and put it in some rice to dry it out." I get that it's gross, but it's not a public toilet and it was flushed.

"You didn't see the way I punished the toilet this morning. There's no way that water isn't teeming with bacteria."

"I've seen you eat a potato chip off the ground."

"It's too gross."

"You had to wipe an ant off of it first," I argue.

"The ant wasn't covered in shit."

"Neither is the phone," I laugh. Judging by the look on his face, he isn't kidding, so I step out of the shower, pluck the phone from the toilet, give it a quick rinse under the shower head and toss it on the sink. "There, you big baby. Go get some rice."

Grinning at me, he says, "Wash your hands again."

"For someone who stuck their finger up my ass last night,

you are awfully germophobic."

His laughter fades as he heads down the hall. By the time I step out of the shower, he's wiping down the phone with an antibacterial wipe. "If it's as waterproof as it's supposed to be, I shouldn't need the rice."

He turns it on and it comes to life with no problem.

"Crisis averted," I announce, dressing quickly. "What would you have done if it was a public toilet?"

"Gotten a new phone. Toilets seriously gross me out. I always get one of the other guys to clean ours." He grabs me around my waist and pulls me to him. "Are you laughing at me?"

"A little. I guess everyone has something that disgusts them like that, though."

He kisses across my shoulder. "Yeah, what's yours?"

"Spit," I reply instantly.

He kisses me, and I close my eyes, savoring the way his tongue explores mine. My hands run around to squeeze his ass, and a small moan slips from my throat. "You don't seem to mind mine."

"Well, if you hock a big one on the sidewalk or something, then we'll have an issue."

He slaps my ass. "Finish getting ready. I made breakfast."

We decide to make a quick shopping trip after we eat, since he still needs a gift for his father. Noble helped me pick out a gift for his mother since I know nothing about her, and the DVR he buys for his father will come from both of us.

We're heading back toward the mall entrance when I see they have just opened the line to get a picture with Santa. Grabbing Noble's arm, I drag him toward Santa. "I want a picture."

Laughing, he humors me.

When Michelle meets us at the restaurant for dinner, she takes her seat with a sigh of relief.

"Long day?" Noble asks.

"The day before the holiday break? All the kids were crazy. They were just counting down the minutes until the end of the day." She grins at me. "What did you two do?"

"We went to the mall, and got our pictures with Santa."

Michelle laughs when I hand her a copy of Noble and me sitting on Santa's lap. "This is amazing. Can I keep it?"

"That one is yours," I agree. "It sounds like we had a better day than you did."

"It had its moments." She chuckles and shakes her head. "I thought it would be an easy day since I had a video for the class to watch."

"Not the birth video!" Noble interrupts.

"Yes, you wuss, the birth video. Childbirth is a natural, beautiful thing."

Noble sips his water and shudders. "I had nightmares for a month. I've never been so glad not to own a vagina."

"Anyway," Michelle continues. "One of my little troublemakers downloaded an app on their phone that let them control the television. I didn't even know that was possible." She sighs. "He waited until the baby had just been delivered, then paused it and hit rewind. The whole class was treated to a view of the baby going back inside the mother. Then he just kept rewinding and forwarding to make the doctor pull the baby out and put it back in over and over."

I'm overcome by laughter just picturing it, and Noble and Michelle join in. "Then the boys got into a discussion about erections and how they often happen without arousal. It led to a ten minute discussion between them about 'no reason boners' and how to hide them."

"I once got hard thinking about tacos. I feel their pain," Noble says.

The rest of the dinner is fun. Everyone is talkative and happy. It's easy to see how close Noble and his mother are, and I love to see him so happy around his family. We spend the whole evening with his mother. She bakes his favorite cookies, and we play Rummy in front of the fireplace until late.

We sleep in the next morning, and wake to the smell of sausage frying.

"Oh, that smells good," I exclaim, stretching, and kicking the covers off of both of us.

"Mom always makes biscuits and gravy on Christmas. And

today is our Christmas, since we'll be at Dad's for the actual one."

Rolling over, I lay on my belly, propping my chin on his stomach. "Is this how you celebrated holidays as a kid?"

"Yeah, they split up when I was a baby. We'd alternate who I spent Christmas with every year, and just celebrate it early with the odd parent out."

There have been times when I wished I knew my father, but sometimes I'm glad I wasn't passed back and forth like so many kids. His hand runs softly down my cheek. "Are you missing your mother?"

"No, not really. We had good holidays when I was younger, but since I grew up and she got sick, we don't do much anyway. This will be good for her."

"Breakfast!" Michelle calls.

Noble grins at me. "Then we open presents."

His enthusiasm is contagious, and we rush to dress and eat, so we can get to the gift exchange.

A fire burns in the fireplace, making the room glow. It's cozy and inviting. The smile on Noble's face is one I haven't seen before, and I realize it's reflecting the quiet joy being with his family brings him.

"Okay, Goose, here is yours. I hope you like it. You aren't the easiest to shop for since you're all grown up now." She sighs. "Too grown up."

Empty nest syndrome must be hitting her hard, and I try to lighten the mood a bit. "Don't worry, he doesn't act his age most of the time."

Michelle smiles at me. "Yeah, I saw the protest video. I assume it was Kenny in the dinosaur suit?"

"We drew straws. He won," Noble chuckles, tearing the paper from the box of work clothing his mother bought for him.

"I thought now that you have a professional job, you probably need some clothes without a draw string or cargo pockets."

"He really does," I remark.

"Hey, no teaming up against me." He leans over to kiss his mom's cheek. "But thank you. I really do need them. I only own one tie."

"And it has the Roadrunner on it," I add, making his mother laugh again.

Noble produces a small box from his pocket. "See, now when you see what I got you, you're going to feel bad for picking on me."

He wiggles like a toddler who has to pee while I open the package. My mouth falls open when I pick up the silver bracelet from the soft padding it's resting on. Two small stars are connected on both sides by smooth, braided silver. I recognize it instantly, but there's no way. It was in such bad shape when we pulled it from the river.

With a soft smile, Noble takes it and fastens it around my wrist. "The jeweler was able to restore it. He could only salvage two of the stars, but I thought that was perfect. You're the bright, shining star I've tried to catch for so long, and the other star is me, sticking to you whether you like it or not."

The bastard made me cry. In front of his mother. Who also has tears in her eyes. My voice cracks as I throw my arms around him and tell him, "I love it. The bracelet, and you sticking to me."

His mother is looking back and forth between us. "Your babies are going to be so adorable. January's dark hair and your blue eyes." She sighs as both Noble and I stare at each other with a terrified look.

"Don't worry. I don't want kids until I'm close to thirty." His body relaxes, and I can't help but giggle. The truth is I never plan to have kids, but there's no way I'm killing the hope in her eyes.

I hand him his gift. "Your mom is right. You aren't the easiest to shop for."

Michelle laughs aloud when he pulls out the hoodie that reads, *I've got your warm front, baby.* Printed on the front is a map of the US, showing the jet stream pushing a warm front across the country. Grinning, he puts it on and shoves his hands in the pockets to find the gift certificate.

It took some researching, but I found a storm chasing team willing to let him ride along with them for a few days in the spring, during prime tornado season. It'll scare the shit out of me, but I know his dream is to see a tornado up close.

His look of shock followed by elation is all I could've hoped for. "This is amazing! Thank you!" He pulls me into his lap and kisses me hard on the lips.

"What is it?" Michelle asks, gathering the wrapping paper and tossing it into the fire.

Noble throws me a quick look then lies through his teeth. "A weekend at a weather camp. Where I can learn from established climatologists."

"How thoughtful!"

"Open yours, Ma. Jani picked it out, so if it sucks, you can blame her."

We both roll our eyes at him, and she opens her gift, an e-reader I've preloaded with a few of her favorite books.

"I know you aren't crazy about technology and stuff, but that will hold thousands of books," Noble explains, reaching over to turn it on. "It has a long lasting battery and can be seen in any light, even outside in the sun."

"Oh, it already has one of my favorites!" she exclaims, noticing the cover.

"More than one," Noble says. "And the gift card will let you get more. Some e-books sell as cheap as a dollar, so you'll never run out of stuff to read when you're bored at work."

"This is great. Thank you so much. You'll have to show me how to use it."

Noble's phone rings, and I see his father's name pop up. "I'll show you how it works. I have one at home and I've nearly worn it out," I volunteer.

Noble gives me a grateful glance and gets to his feet, answering the call as he leaves the room.

Michelle sits beside me on the couch as I show her everything the e-reader can do. We spend a few minutes searching the bookstore and buying a few new ones she had on her wish list. "If you take it to your local library, they can also show you how to borrow e-books for free as well. I haven't tried that yet, but I know there's a way."

"My friend works at the library, so I'm sure she can show me." She pauses and looks at me for a moment. "Noble is in love with you."

Whoa. Where did that come from?

"I-I don't know about that."

A smile blooms across her face. "I do. He loves you and it's a joy to see." Her head tilts and she appears to consider her next question a moment before asking it. "Do you love him?"

Wow, way to put me on the spot. "I don't know," I answer honestly. "I've never been in love before. I don't know how it's supposed to feel."

She nods, and pats me on the knee. "You're young. I remember being your age when everything was bright and new, so many possibilities. I thought I'd outgrown all that until I met Bruce. But apparently you don't outgrow that fluttery feeling in your stomach when they look at you, or the way the silliest things they say can make you laugh."

"Noble always makes me laugh. He's so much fun to be with. We've pretty much spent all our free time together over the last month. I mean, sometimes, I want to choke him, but most of the time, I just want to be near him."

Michelle laughs. "I can understand that."

Looking to make sure he isn't lurking nearby, I add, "When I wake up, the first thing I want to do is talk to him. If he isn't there, it's like my day doesn't start until I hear from him. It scares me a little," I confess. "I don't want to be too clingy. Is that love?"

"That's something you'll have to decide for yourself. Falling in love throws you into a whole new world. Things look different, brighter. The little struggles and massive problems aren't so hard to deal with when you can lie in the arms of someone who loves you."

She stops talking when Noble returns, and I hug her. "I'll keep that in mind, thanks."

Noble eyes us with suspicion. "What were you talking about?"

"She was just warning me about your occasional bed wetting problem. Don't worry, I can deal with it."

Betrayal sweeps over his face, and he gapes at his mother. "That hasn't happened since I was seventeen! Okay, one time last year, but I was drunk!"

The room is dead quiet for a second before it fills with laughter. "I was kidding," I choke out between giggles. "I was just talking about books she might like."

It sinks in that he's told on himself and he shrugs. "I was kidding too."

Turning to his mother, I ask, "Do you think we should believe him?"

"I don't know. I guess it all Depends." We dissolve into laughter again, and he grins, shaking his head.

"Putting you two together was a really bad idea."

We leave his mother's house in the late afternoon and head for his dad's in Indiana. The sparkling bracelet on my wrist keeps catching my eye, and Michelle's words ring in my ears. My world is different, brighter with Noble in it. Maybe I am falling for him.

When Noble's father answers the door, it's clear where Noble gets his good looks. I have a feeling I'm seeing what Noble will look like when he's in his forties.

"Well, who is this pretty young thing and how did you get her to come with you?"

"Bribery, mostly," I joke. "I'm January. It's nice to meet you."

"Todd," he replies, leading us into the house. "It's good to meet you too. Noble told me he was bringing a girl, but I figured she'd be plastic. He doesn't have the sex appeal of his old man." His teasing smile is returned by Noble.

"Says the man who wears a tee shirt with Honorary Cock Gobbler written on it."

"It was a gift," he defends.

They stare at each other for a minute, then Todd grabs him in a big bear hug. "It's good to see you, kid."

"You too, Dad. Where's Ben?"

"Work. He'll be here for dinner."

Noble explained on the drive that Ben is Todd's new husband. They got married last year right after the law passed allowing gay marriage. The way Todd beams when he speaks of him, it's clear the honeymoon period hasn't passed.

"Working through the holidays? That sucks," Noble remarks.

"Lots of slips and falls, kids breaking bones on their new toys, stuff like that this time of year. He's pretty busy."

"Your husband is a doctor?" I ask.

Todd takes my coat as he answers me, hanging it in a nearby closet. "He's an orthopedist. That's how we met. I work in transcription, and I had to call to check on some of his notes before transcribing them. Doctors are known for poor handwriting, but he pushes the limit. Never saw such chicken scratch in my life."

We settle on the couch in the living room and spend the next hour talking and getting to know each other.

Todd stares at his phone for a moment before jumping to his feet and racing out of the room. Noble returns my quizzical look, and is just about to follow him when he returns.

"Sorry, there was a Butterfree in the kitchen. I've been trying to catch one of those little bastards all week."

"A butterfly?" How the hell does he have a butterfly in the house when it's about thirty degrees outside?

"I've got one," Noble replies smugly.

"Well, I have a Charizard."

A moment of silence ensues before I announce. "Well, I have no clue what you two are talking about."

They both laugh, and Noble shows me his phone where he has loaded a game. "Pokemon Go. I'm beating his ass and he can't accept it."

Todd smirks. "It's a nice evening. Maybe you'd like to take a little walk and show your girl around town."

"Where's the closest gym?"

"The old high school. The park down the street is a Pokestop."

Noble turns to me. "Is it too cold out for you?"

"No, I'm fine. But just to get this straight, we're going to walk around so you can catch cartoon animals?"

Todd chuckles and smiles at me. "When you say it like that, it just sounds ridiculous."

"We're also going to fight them so I can takeover the gym for the blue team," Noble defends.

"Whatever blows your skirt up, babe," I reply.

I guess we're hunting for Pokemon.

We get ready to go, and I'm already bundled up when Noble wraps a thick scarf around my neck and drops a kiss on my lips. "If you get too cold, tell me, okay?"

"I will."

Noble drives us a few blocks away and parks beside a small playground. I'm shocked at the amount of people I see roaming around the play equipment and sitting on the picnic tables in the chilly darkness.

By the time we're out of the car, Noble and Todd are staring at their phones with matching grins, and I realize all these people are doing the same thing as them. "There was an update today," Noble explains. "New Pokemon and stuff."

I thought it was a bit weird at first, but watching Noble and his father race around, laughing and smiling, may be the most adorable thing I've ever seen. There are so many people here, and most are obviously strangers to each other, but you wouldn't know it by watching them. They are all so excited about the game. They talk to each other, helping one another get ahead. It's not often you see a sixty-year-old man approach a group of teens with more holes pierced in them than a pasta strainer, and then watch them work together to achieve some goal in the game. It's touching in an odd sort of way.

When they've done all they can here, we all walk down the street to what Noble refers to as a gym. It's actually an abandoned high school, and I'm betting this is the most visitors it has seen since it was closed down. People are seated in small groups on the lawn, fighting their Pokemon to win for their team.

"I'm going to stand by the fire," I tell Noble, giving him a quick kiss. "Go kick some ass."

Grinning, he and his father take off and join a group of four kids sitting on the stone steps.

A large fire roars in an oversized portable fire pit that I assume someone has dragged out here. Three older women—well, older than me—stand around it, rubbing their hands together and talking. I can't make out much, except their faces since they're bundled up as much as I am.

I'm graced with a smile from one of them when I approach—who I mentally dub as Red Hat, since she's wearing, you guessed it, a red hat—and the others give me a nod as they continue their conversation.

"It's just so ridiculous," the woman in a horribly ugly scarf says. "But, they're kids, you know. It's a fad that'll pass."

Red Hat's head bobs and she moves closer to the fire. "At least the other games could be played in their bedrooms, and I didn't have to drive them all over town."

The third woman, who wears a killer pair of calf high boots, speaks up. "My Harry expected me to let him walk all the way here with just his friends, no adult supervision whatsoever! It's almost half a mile and they're only twelve. Just because the other mothers don't care if their kids get kidnapped doesn't mean I'm risking mine." She glances around to locate a boy I instantly feel sorry for. Helicopter parents are the worst.

Red hat turns to me. "Did you hear about the man who walked right off of a cliff while playing this game?"

Swallowing back a laugh, I shake my head. "I never heard of the game until today."

"Another man stopped his truck in the middle of the highway and caused a multi car pile-up. Can you imagine? A grown man doing that over a stupid game." Ugly Scarf tuts. She looks around and drops her voice as if the players might hear her. "Of course, there are some adults here without children. I guess the virgins have to crawl out of their mother's basements for something."

All three women cackle, and it makes me think of that witch from Looney Tunes. The one who leaves bobby pins in the air. I can never remember her name.

They go on like that for a while, and I just listen. They're so judgmental I want to smack them. After a few minutes, Killer

Boots turns to me. "That's my little Harry over by the steps. Which one is yours?"

Noble and his father are making their way toward me, and I gesture to them. "Here comes mine now, with his father. Hey, babe!" I wave, and the expression on Noble's face says he knows I'm up to something.

I throw my arms around him. "Hi, did you have fun? I know it's colder out here than in your mom's basement. And the moonlight is awfully bright."

His expression is quizzical, but he plays along. "Yeah, but we should get back soon, or you never know what could happen."

"What is the name of the witch on Looney Tunes?" I ask, and Todd answers.

"Hazel?"

"Yes! That's it. It was driving me crazy."

Todd is looking at me like I might already be crazy. "Why were you trying to think of the witch's name?"

"Oh." I meet the gaze of each woman before replying, "Just met some people who reminded me of her."

Pulling Noble closer to me, I give his ass a squeeze. "Are you ready to go get rid of that pesky virginity now?"

Todd bursts out laughing while Noble just shakes his head.

"Yours or mine?"

"Hell, let's just get rid of both." Turning around, I pull my hat down over my ears. "See you later, ladies, I have a basement dweller to deflower."

Todd beams at me, then his son. "This one is a keeper, boy."

Chapter Seven

Noble

January managed to win over both of my parents in less than three days. I'm pretty sure they like her more than me, since they both warn me not to blow it. After our Pokemon hunt, we spend the night watching movies with Dad.

It's late when we finally go to bed, but we don't get much sleep. The sun has just made an appearance when Jani's phone rings. She groans, rolls over, grabs it from the night stand and mumbles, "Hello?"

A split second later, she's sitting ramrod straight. "What? When? Is she okay?"

All the blood drains from her face, and I run my hand down her back, trying to comfort her without interrupting. "I shouldn't have let her go alone." She pauses, listening to the caller. "I'm not home. I'm with my boyfriend, just north of Indianapolis."

She turns to me and pretends to draw on the air. Nodding, I rush to get her a pen and paper. "Yeah, I've got it," she says, jotting down a few lines. "Just text me the gate info and everything."

When she finally hangs up, I wrap her in my arms. "What happened?"

"It's Mom. They think she had a stroke. They had to call an

ambulance."

"I'm so sorry. What can I do?"

"My aunt and uncle are arranging a flight for me from the Indianapolis airport. Can you get me there?"

"Of course I can." My mind spins with what else I should be doing. I've never really been faced with an emergency like this. "Get dressed and I'll warm up the car."

I leave her to get ready and step into my dad's room. He and Ben are already awake. "What's going on?" Dad asks.

"Jani's mom had a stroke. I guess it doesn't look good. She's going to catch a flight out of Indianapolis to Hawaii." I run my hands through my hair as Dad follows me out to the hall. "I don't know what to do. I should go with her, but…"

"Do you have any idea how much a last minute ticket to Hawaii two days before Christmas would be? If you can even get a seat?"

"I know." Even if I depleted my savings, I wouldn't be able to swing it. I know Dad struggles too or he'd loan me the money.

His hands land on my shoulders. "Just get her to the airport and make sure she gets on the plane okay. Do you want me to go with you?"

"No, no, I got it. I just hate she has to go alone."

"Does she have family to meet her?"

"Yeah, they paid for her ticket."

"Then she'll be okay. It sucks, I know, not being able to stay with her, but you do what you can."

By the time I get the car warmed up, Jani is packed and ready to go. She holds my hand the entire drive to Indianapolis, and right up until it's time to board the plane. Watching her leave by herself makes me feel completely helpless and I hate it.

When I get back to my car, I just need to talk to someone.

"Noble?" Denton yawns out my name as he answers his phone. "You okay?"

"Yeah. No. Fuck man, I don't know. I just dropped Jani off at the airport. Her mother had a stroke and she had to fly to her aunt's in Hawaii."

"Oh, dude. That sucks. Do they know if she'll be okay?"

"I don't think they know much of anything yet. I just feel like an asshole because I didn't go with her. I just couldn't afford it."

"Man, none of us could. Don't beat yourself up over it."

"Have the other guys left town yet?"

"Yeah, they left last night."

Sighing, I turn on the car and crank up the heat. "I'm going to stop by my Dad's and then head back that way."

"I'll be here."

Dad is more than understanding about me leaving early. I may not be able to be with her, but I want to be there when she gets home. She promised to call me as soon as the plane lands, but it's nearly an eight-hour flight, so I'm back home at my apartment by the time she texts.

Jani: Aunt just picked me up from the airport. On our way to hospital.

Me: I'm sorry I'm not there with you. Please let me know how Aubrey is doing when you can. Take care of yourself.

Jani: I will. Apologize to your dad for me.

Me: He understands.

Denton is the only one home and after watching me pace the apartment for an hour, he hands me a glass of whiskey. "Sit down. You aren't helping by wearing out the tile. Fuck knows these cheap ass floors can't take it."

When I sit, he hands me a stack of stapled together papers. "Here, take your mind off Jani. We have another problem to deal with. This was left on the door yesterday."

The first page is a letter from the housing management announcing the apartment complex has been bought by a new company. While they will remain income based and rent won't increase, they have new rules and regulations. They make it clear multiple times that breaking them can result in eviction.

Shit. I knew things were going too well.

I flip through the pages, then gape at Denton. "Are they serious with this shit?"

"It's legit. I called to make sure it wasn't a joke."

Monthly inspections where they come to judge your housework? Anyone without a job must volunteer ten hours a week with their company? "Is this shit even legal?" I ask.

"I've been researching, and they run complexes in other cities the same way. I don't know about legal, but does it really matter? No one here could afford to challenge them anyway."

I've never been one to feel sorry for myself for not being financially stable. I mean, so many are worse off than I am, and most students are in a similar situation. I know it's not forever so I don't dwell on it. But this is the first time I've really felt poor. In one day, I've gained two problems that could've been greatly helped by having money. I swear, once I've graduated and work full time, I'll sock away every dime I can.

"I was discussing it with some of the other neighbors," Denton says and a wicked grin creeps across his face. "We have a plan. A little malicious compliance."

"Like?"

"Well, being naked in your own apartment isn't against the rules, so bring on the inspections. Half the circle has already agreed to go balls to the wind."

Denton grins when I laugh. I can't help picturing some of my neighbors, who are all sizes and ages, just running bare assed around the house as someone checks to see if we've mopped our floors. "This is crazy."

"Yeah, I mean, didn't they see the response when the town tried to close Scarlet Toys? You'd think they'd learn not to mess with us, but we're just going to have to show them."

My phone rings with a call from Cassidy. Shit, I should've called her. She's Jani's best friend, so I'm sure she's let her know.

"Noble, get your shit together. You've got a flight on a private plane to Hawaii in an hour."

"What the hell are you smoking?" I ask, getting to my feet. The guys always screw with me because I can't sit still when I'm on the phone.

"Look, we're headed there too, but it's going to take us longer to get there, and Jani needs someone with her. You're the boyfriend, so get your shit together and get to the Morganville Airport."

"Don't you think I wanted to go with her? I don't have the money!"

Cass sighs. "Are you dense? There are times when being engaged to a gazillionaire comes in handy. This is one of them. Get your ass to Hawaii. Bring Denton if you want. I know he's alone for Christmas."

"I—" This is one of those times when my pride isn't as important as someone I care about, so I swallow it and accept. "Thank you. Tell Wyatt I'll pay him back."

She snorts into the phone. "Shut the fuck up and get moving."

Denton and I perform the fastest packing job in history and race to the tiny airport where we board a plane that looks like it could be brought down by a large bird. I'm not sure you could even call this little illuminated strip of pavement an airport.

Denton's glance is full of amusement. "Are you scared to fly?"

"No, I just didn't think the first time would be in a glorified remote-controlled plane."

Chuckling, Denton hands me a pill just after I buckle myself in. "It's what I take for anxiety. It'll calm you down."

Calm me down? I swallow the pill, grit my teeth through the takeoff, and pass the fuck out. Denton has to shake me awake as we're descending.

"Hey, lightweight, wake up. We're landing."

I'm instantly sorry when I look out the window and see the ground advancing toward us. "You couldn't wait another few minutes?"

"And miss that look on your face?" He laughs, and I breathe a sigh of relief when the plane rolls to a stop.

"I hope you get a spontaneous bout of severe diarrhea."

We disembark and find a car waiting to take us to the hospital. "We have to find a way to thank Wyatt and Cass for all this," I tell Denton.

"They're awesome friends to have," he agrees. "It's

beautiful here."

It's such an abrupt change from the winter hellscape we just left.

Even the hospital looks bright and welcoming, surrounded by palm trees and landscaped grounds. A large courtyard sprinkled with benches is host to quite a few people. Some are patients, dressed in pajamas and towing their IV poles along with them.

We're cutting through the courtyard when I see her out of the corner of my eye. I'd know that dark hair and those amazing hips anywhere. My chest loosens a bit when I see her mother sitting on the bench, wearing a robe. They're both talking and wearing identical smiles.

In retrospect, I probably should've given some thought to the way I approached her. If you're picturing that romantic run across the lawn into each other's arms, forget it.

Walking up behind her, I sling my arm around her neck and murmur, "Hey sexy, you come here often?"

At least, that's what I was trying to say. I only get the first four words out before my foot is stomped on like it's a damned grape. A split second later, the wind is forced from my lungs by an elbow to my solar plexus, and my lip swells as her fist makes contact incredibly fast.

Dropping onto the soft grass, I try to inhale and only get that braying donkey sound. "What the—Noble?" she exclaims.

Drawing a thin breath, I nod, and I'm vaguely aware of Denton laughing his ass off behind me.

"What are you doing here?"

I finally manage to fill my lungs and stumble to my feet, one of which feels like a puffer fish. "Surprise," I squeak. "I was worried about you and Aubrey. Wyatt arranged a flight for us."

"Your girl whooped your ass!" Denton announces, still laughing. "Oh, why wasn't I recording?"

"I'm so sorry! It was a reflex!" Jani steps forward and wraps her arms around me. She also manages to step on the same foot she tried to pulverize a moment before.

"Sorry!" she repeats while Denton tries to laugh himself

into a hernia.

"Let's just...sit for a minute, okay?" I take a seat beside her mom. "How are you?"

Aubrey smiles, looking a bit embarrassed. "It wasn't a stroke. It was an MS attack. They're easy to mistake. They've adjusted my meds a bit, and I'm feeling much better. I just have to stay a few days for observation."

January sits on my other side, her smile as bright as the day. "I can't believe you're here."

It's been less than forty-eight hours since we saw each other, but she hugs me like she hasn't seen me in months. It's the first time I've felt like maybe she feels as strongly for me as I do for her.

"It was really sweet of you to come," Aubrey adds.

"Hey, what about me? I had to deal with Mr. Afraid of Planes over there."

"I'm not afraid of planes."

"Not once they land."

Aubrey laughs and gets to her feet carefully. "I'm just going to the next bench to chat with Helen. Hang out with your friends, honey." She meets up with a plump older lady walking toward her, and they take a seat out of earshot.

Turning to Jani, I pretend to whisper. "He drugged me, baby. Probably took advantage and touched my no-no spot while I was sleeping."

My joke gets the laughter I was hoping for. It's good to see her happy after the way she looked when she left.

"You have to enjoy the little things in life," Denton says, looking around. "Is there a vending machine or anything around here. I'm starving."

"Just inside the emergency department doors," Jani tells him, and he jogs off in search of food.

A gust of wind wraps her hair around her face, and I tuck it back behind her ear. "Are you okay?"

"Yeah, much better now. I was just getting ready to call you when—"

"You assaulted me?" I tease.

"Hey, any guy who grabs me from behind is going to get his ass kicked. That's just how it is."

She leans against me, and I sit back, soaking in the sun. "Where did you learn that?"

"Women's self-defense class. Cass and I went last year."

"Well, thank you for not going for the jewels."

Giggling, she plants a kiss on my sore lip. "Did I hurt you?"

"Nah." I just won't be able to take my shoe off because there's no way it'll go back on. "So, your Mom is okay?"

Shrugging, she cuddles against me. "No worse than usual, but I'm worried about her. I think she wants to stay here, like move here permanently."

Fear streaks through me, but I try to sound unconcerned. "Would you move with her?"

"No, my life is in Indiana. You, my friends, my job. I'm not leaving. I'm just not sure what's best for her, you know? My aunt and uncle are seriously loaded, and they love her. I'm sure they could take better care of her."

"What does Aubrey want?"

Sighing, she glances over to where her mother and aunt are laughing together. "I think she wants to stay. I'm just worried she's doing it to take the burden off of me. She knows if I wasn't paying all our expenses, buying her meds and paying for the therapy that insurance won't cover, I could get ahead, maybe take the classes I've been wanting to take. If she thinks she'd be happier here, I understand, but I don't want her moving here just to help me."

Aubrey and Helen walk up, and Helen sticks out her hand. "Hi, I'm Helen. I've heard all about you, Noble. It was sweet of you to come. Seems your name is apt."

"It's nice to meet you."

"Well, I was just telling Aubrey, you and your friend can stay with January in the east wing." She gestures to the two suitcases we left sitting beside the parking lot. "Is that all your luggage?"

"Yes, ma'am, we didn't have much time to pack, but we can get a hotel room. Denton has already reserved one near the hospital."

"Don't be silly. We have more than enough room!"

Considering her house has wings, I don't doubt that.

"Thank you, Aunt Helen," Jani intervenes.

"I'm just going to rest for the remainder of the day," Aubrey says. "You should take him to the beach, Jani. Show him around."

"But—"

Her mother gives her a look. "I'm fine. And I promise to call if that changes. It's your Christmas holiday. Go enjoy it."

A car stops near our bags in the parking lot and Cass and Wyatt emerge.

"Oh yeah, I forgot to tell you. Cassidy and Wyatt are coming."

I swear Jani tears up and this is not a girl who ever cries. I guess having your best friends show up thousands of miles away on Christmas Eve is enough to do it.

"I'm going to go find Denton," I murmur. "We'll catch up with you okay?"

She nods and runs toward Cassidy. I watch as they hug. "See, that's the reunion we should've had," I mumble to myself, and Aubrey cracks up laughing.

Denton stands just outside the hospital, sucking down a soda and a bag of chips. "Come on, dude. We're staying with Jani's family."

"Okay, then."

"Holy hell, your family lives here?" Denton exclaims when we pull up to a sprawling mansion overlooking the ocean.

"My aunt and uncle," she clarifies. "And my cousins, Chloe and Brinna. They're both home for the holidays too, so you'll probably meet them. They're in another wing, though."

Jani shows us around the place, and it's unbelievable. Seven bathrooms for four people? We had to arm wrestle for the room with the attached bath at my apartment, and I was thrilled not to have to share the only other bathroom with three guys and the revolving door of women they bring home.

This place is better than a resort. An inground pool is just a few steps out the back door, complete with a waterfall and diving boards. I don't know why they'd want a pool when they're this close to the beach, but it does look inviting. A long staircase leads down to the white sand of a private beach where a woman in a bikini walks along the waterline.

"There's a reef over there I always liked to explore when I was a kid," Jani says, pointing to the right. "We can go snorkeling if you want."

Denton is like a kid in an amusement park. "Yes! I'd love to snorkel. I brought swim trunks, but I don't have goggles or a snorkel or anything."

Jani shows us into the pool house. "These two are changing rooms, and the third room is full of trunks, swimsuits, goggles, anything you need. They won't mind what you borrow. I'm going to get changed and I'll be right back."

When I emerge from one of the dressing rooms wearing a new pair of board shorts, and carrying goggles and a snorkel, Denton is waiting for me with a huge smile on his face. "Dude! This is so amazing! Jani's mom is okay, and we got a Hawaiian vacation out of the deal."

We walk out on the deck, and he doesn't take his eyes off of the ocean as Jani approaches us carrying three sets of fins. "It's so blue," he murmurs.

Jani leans against me and sighs. "Beautiful, isn't it?"

"It's so much more…powerful than it looks on television."

Jani turns to Denton. "Have you never seen the ocean?"

"No, my family didn't really take vacations."

Of course they didn't. I struggle with money for the reason a lot of people my age do, because we're trying to pay for college. Sometimes I forget that Denton grew up a lot worse off than I did. I may not have had everything I wanted, but I didn't do without anything growing up.

"Come on," Jani says, smiling at him. "You have to see what

warm sand between your toes feels like."

It really is something special to watch someone experience a beach for the first time. We run around and goof off like a bunch of little kids, splashing in the surf. It turns out Denton isn't a strong swimmer, and after he realizes how hard the waves pull at you, even with a life vest, he's too nervous to swim out as far as the reef, so he stays on the shore while we snorkel.

"I feel kind of bad leaving him," she worries as we make our way out to the reef.

"He's fine. Look at him." He's playing in the sand, probably building a castle. He's managed to find a kid's pail that was abandoned and is filling it with water and heading back to his project.

It's getting late and the sun rests low in the sky, throwing sparkles across the water's surface and January's face. It's one of those moments I know I'll remember forever, watching the sunlight dance across her smile.

"Look down," she says.

I stick the snorkel in my mouth and do as she says. As I said, I've swam in an ocean before, but I've never seen anything like this. I didn't expect the colors to be so vibrant. A huge, green sea turtle swims right beneath me, and I watch transfixed as a rainbow of tropical fish dart in and out of the vast array of vegetation.

We stay out there until the sun starts to set and the wind begins to pick up. I'm just about to ask Jani if she's ready to go back when I see a small jellyfish swimming next to me. I've never seen one close up. It's so weird looking, I want to show Jani, but I know better than to grab it and get stung.

Isn't it only the tentacles that sting? This one is tiny, so I have an idea that I'm soon going to regret. Taking off my goggles, I scoop up the jellyfish. It falls into the space effortlessly and it doesn't look like it can climb out or anything.

"What are you doing?" Jani asks.

"Look, I caught a jellyfish." She swims toward the shore when I start toward her.

"Are you crazy? Those little bastards hurt. My uncle had to

pee on my cousin once to stop the pain when he got stung. Chuck it away from you and let's go before it gets dark."

"Aww, he just wants a little kiss, Jani. Look how cute he is," I taunt. A wave sweeps over us and washes the jellyfish out of the goggles. "Oh shit! I don't know where it is!" I call, throwing the goggles back on and swimming like hell toward the shore. I can hear January's laughter ahead of me.

It isn't until I'm wading up the shore that I realize I've made a mistake. A huge, horrible, burning mistake.

"Shit, that hurts!" I curse, flinging off the goggles.

Jani's jaw drops. "You put the goggles back on? Jesus Chalupa Christ, Noble! They must be covered in stinging cells!"

She rushes up to me. "Did they get into your eyes or is it just the skin around them?"

"I don't think it got in my eyes." I move my hands away and she gasps. Definitely not a good sign.

"You need to see a doctor."

"On Christmas Eve?" I scoff. "No way. And my insurance isn't going to pay when we're out of state."

"Fuck, dude," Denton exclaims. "I don't think you have a choice."

The pain is unbelievable, and my eyes start to pour. The salty tears set the irritated skin on fire. Splashing water across my face doesn't help since it's just as salty.

Jani turns to Denton. "You've got to pee on him."

Denton shakes his head, taking a step back.

"It's what you're supposed to do for a jellyfish sting. It stops the burning."

"I know that, but…"

Turning my head away from them, I top off the stellar moment by throwing up. "Sorry," I groan. "The pain is turning my stomach."

"You do it," Denton tells Jani.

"How?" she snaps. "You expect me to me just strip, squat, and piss on him?"

"I can't golden shower my best friend!"

Stumbling back onto the sandy shore, I plop onto the sand.

My face is swollen to the point where I can't see much, but I can hear them arguing about what to do.

"Just take this pail and fill it up. I'll turn my back," Denton says.

All my pride flies right out the window. I never imagined a jellyfish sting could hurt like this. I was stung on the arm when I was young and it wasn't like this. Of course, my face would be more sensitive. "Please, Jani," I mumble.

"Okay, but when we get back, I'm calling a doctor."

"Deal." I'd say anything at this point. I mean, once you reach the point where splashing piss on your face sounds like a good option, you don't have much left to lose.

"Denton, I swear if you turn around and peek, I'll kick you in the head until my hip dislocates," Jani warns.

Amusement is clear in Denton's voice when he replies, "Understood."

I lie back on the sand and the sound of Jani peeing into the bucket is briefly drowned out by Denton's chuckle. I'm never going to live this shit down.

"Give me your shirt," she tells Denton. "I'm not just going to dump it on him."

"Okay, babe," Jani says. "Just stay still, okay?"

"Yeah."

A second later the damp cloth lands just above my eye and the relief is almost instant. "It's helping," I breathe.

"Good. Now keep your mouth shut unless you want a taste."

"Not that we're judging if you do," Denton adds, and I flip the bird in the direction of his voice.

The pain is now manageable, so I take the shirt from Jani and stand up, holding it to my face. Jani holds my arm, leading me back up the path and stairs to the mansion. She starts a shower while Denton grabs me some clean clothes. I can hear her on her phone as I'm washing away the sand and grime from the beach. I can't use soap on my face, but a quick rinse with cool water feels good and gets rid of the "I just got pissed on" smell.

"Aunt Helen said we should just go to the emergency

room."

"The pain is better now. I might be able to wait it out."

I don't have to see her to know her arms are crossed and the little wrinkle on her forehead is standing out. "Your eyes are swollen shut and you have no idea if you've damaged your vision. Unless you want to be reading next year's textbooks in braille, we're going to the hospital."

"Fine, let's go."

This is not how I pictured my holiday going.

Chapter Eight

January

After a few hours in the ER, an IV of steroids to fight the inflammation, and a quick check by an ophthalmologist, Noble is finally okay to go home. Luckily, his vision wasn't permanently affected. As soon as the swelling goes down, he'll be able to see normally again.

When we return to my aunt's home, Denton is lounging in the living room with my cousins. Brinna is preoccupied with her phone, but Chloe is practically in his lap, laughing over something he just said.

"Hey, what did the doctor say?" Denton asks.

"I'm okay," Noble says, then proceeds to walk into the coffee table.

Denton snorts. "Yeah, you seem perfectly fine."

"He will be once the swelling goes down," I explain.

"You'll be happy to know you've been awarded the dumbass of the month award. Kenny and Trey agree. It's no contest."

Noble curses and glares in Denton's direction. "What did you do, call them the second we left?"

"Of course not. I texted. It's Christmas Eve, after all. I don't want to interrupt those with a normal family life."

I take Noble's arm as he flips him off.

"I'm a little farther to the right," Denton laughs. "I know *urine* a bad mood, but there's no reason to get *pissy* with me."

Chloe giggles and moves closer to Denton. I can't help the chuckle that escapes me, and Noble turns to me.

His lips twitch up as he asks, "Are you laughing at me?"

"Of course not, babe. I'm laughing with you."

"I'm not laughing."

Denton pipes up again. "Aw, don't be such a wet towel...I mean blanket."

I know they'll go on all night like this if I let them. "Aunt Helen said Christmas Eve dinner will be at seven. She'll be back by then. Denton, are you okay on your own for a bit longer while I get Noble taken care of?"

"I think I'm in good hands." He winks at Chloe.

"I'll see you at dinner then."

Wrapping my arm around Noble's, I lead him back to our room. He falls onto the bed with a sigh. I know he must feel miserable with the drugs they gave him and everything, and I feel bad because none of this would have happened if he hadn't come here after me. Fortunately, I know just the thing to cheer him up.

"I think I'll skip the dinner," he says. "I just need a nap."

A small smile graces his lips when he feels me pull his shoes off. "The door is locked. You can get comfortable. I'll grab you a cool compress for your eyes."

"Thanks," he mumbles.

When I return from the bathroom, he's lying on his back in only a pair of boxers.

Perfect.

He turns his head toward me when I sit on the bed beside him. "Can you see at all?"

"If I raise my eyebrows and open my eyes wide, but it's sore." He runs his hand down my back. "Go join the others, Jan. It's Christmas Eve. And I'm just going to fall asleep."

"I will. After I take care of you." My hand slides down over his crotch as I speak. His cock instantly jumps to life. I swear, most men could be on their deathbed and still perk up at the first sign of a blow job.

I drape the cool cloth across his eyes and press a soft kiss to his lips.

"If this turns out to be some drug-soaked dream and I'm still at the hospital for jellyfish poisoning, I'm going to be super angry."

His joking comes to a halt when I lick down his neck and chest, pausing to pay attention to his nipples since he really seems to like that. His breath catches when I nip at them, and he groans. "God, yes, babe. Bite them."

His cock is rock hard and dripping by the time I pull down his boxers. Being unable to see me must really add to the sensation for him because he looks like he could come any second. "Ooooh fuck," he groans, when I deliver a long, gentle lick from his balls to the head.

This is one area where I'm completely confident. The trick to giving a good blow job is simple. While different guys like different things, they all appreciate enthusiasm. You've got to go after that cock like you've been brainwashed by it, like all you can ever think about is getting it in your mouth again.

Knowing his dominant tendencies in bed, I grab his hand and put it on the back of my head, giving him the illusion of control, and then I really get into it. The gasps and hisses, groans and cursing just drives me on. His thighs tighten and relax, and I love the way he loses control when he gets close.

Pausing for a second, I ask, "In my mouth or on my tits?"

The words alone seem to shove him to the edge and he gasps out, "Tits."

I sit up and rub his cock between my breasts. It takes about three seconds for him to come, and his hands instantly begin to rub it over my nipples. "God, January, you are fucking perfect."

Yeah, I thought he'd like that.

After I get us cleaned up, he's snoring like a congested walrus, so I pull the covers over him and creep out of the room. Those antihistamines they gave him will probably keep him out for the night.

Aunt Helen, Brinna, Chloe, and Denton all wait at the table, which is covered with platters of food.

"January, dear, I'm glad you could join us. How is your friend?" Aunt Helen smiles at me as the food starts getting passed around the table.

"He's feeling better. The meds knocked him out. He asked me to apologize for all the trouble and thank you for having us."

She flips a hand at us. "Nonsense. You're both more than welcome. I don't get to see nearly enough of you and your mother. I'm glad to have you here under any circumstances."

See, Aunt Helen is just the kindest person in the world. I've truly never met another person like her, and I have no idea how she ended up with my asshat of an uncle. "It's good to see you too. Mom often talks about visiting, but it isn't so easy for her to travel anymore." I take a sip of water. "Where is Uncle Leon?" Not that I give a fart in a windstorm where he is or what he's doing, but it seemed polite to ask.

I'm met with a forced smile. "He had some business to take care of."

The food is wonderful, and the conversation stays light and cheerful. Near the end of the meal, I accidentally bump my spoon with my elbow, knocking it to the floor. When I retrieve it, my eyes encounter something I definitely could have lived without.

My cousin Chloe's dress ends just past her hips, and apparently, she doesn't consider panties essential. Razors aren't a necessity either, judging by the panty hamster that's staring back at me. I grab the spoon and raise my head back up, but not quickly enough to avoid the sight of Denton's hand crawling toward the afrogina.

Gross.

Gross.

Double Gross.

Denton gives me a wicked smile when I surface and set the spoon aside. Doing my best to ignore them and the shudder inducing sight I've just endured, I turn to Aunt Helen. "Would it be all right if I made a plate for Mom? I'll run it to the hospital."

"What a thoughtful idea. I'll go with you. Would you like

dessert first?"

"No thank you. I'm stuffed. I'll just check on Noble, first."

Noble is curled up, deeply asleep, and I swear, he's so damn adorable like this. The puffiness around his eyes has gone down a lot, so he'll probably feel much better when he wakes. I throw the blanket over him and sneak back out the door.

Aunt Helen and I arrive at the hospital, and wave to the nurses as we make our way back to Mom's room. Her face lights up when she sees us.

"We brought you a plate. Even in paradise, I can't imagine hospital food is too tasty."

"Cardboard with salt and pepper," she laughs, taking the plate and digging in while Aunt Helen and I sit on the little couch beside her.

After a few minutes of talk and laughter, Mom gives me that look. You know, the one all parent's get when they have something to tell you that you aren't going to like. Aunt Helen takes the hint and excuses herself from the room.

"Jani, honey, I've made a decision. You know Helen has asked me to move in with them, and I've decided to do it. It's so beautiful here. Sunshine and warm temperatures all the time."

My chest tightens, but I do my best not to show my disappointment. "I want you to be wherever will make you happy. Just…I've got everything under control, Mom. Don't do it because you think it's too hard for me."

She gives me a small smile. "January, I know you can do anything you put your mind to. This isn't about you. I'm not trying to lessen your burdens. I honestly think this would be the right choice for me." She glances toward the door, making sure Helen isn't near. "It'll be good for Helen too. Do not tell her I told you this, but she is getting ready to file for divorce, and she's lonely. She needs a support system, and we can lean on one another."

Holy shit. I didn't see that one coming.

"She's divorcing Leon? Is that why he wasn't at Christmas Eve dinner?"

Mom's lips thin in anger. "He's cheating with some

waitress."

"Oh no. That son of a bitch. I hope she takes him for all he has."

Mom bursts out laughing. "That's the plan. There's no prenup, and she has video proof of adultery. He'll be lucky to come out of it with his clothes and car."

My heart aches for Aunt Helen. Nodding, I squeeze Mom's hand. "Okay, if this is where you want to be, I'm not going to argue with you. Just know that you can always change your mind."

Aunt Helen returns, and we spend a few minutes discussing the best ways to ship Mom's things. There's no reason for her to go back when traveling is so hard for her. We finally say goodbye and as we make our way back to the car, Aunt Helen assures me, "I'll take good care of her."

I give her a hug. "I know you will. You're my favorite aunt, you know."

"I'm your only aunt," she snorts.

"Still…"

Laughing, we head back to her home.

Noble is sitting up in bed when I return, looking a bit better, if not a little groggy. "Hey, how do you feel?"

"Better. I can see you," he says with a grin. "Did I miss anything?"

"Do you think you can eat? I'll make you a plate and fill you in. There's an image in my head that I should not have to suffer alone."

"Ooh, I'm intrigued. And starving." He slaps my ass when I bend over to pick up the towel beside the bed. "Fetch me my food and make with the gossip, wench."

"Are you trying to get pissed on again?"

His lips twitch. "That will never be spoken of again."

"Please, your friends will never let it go. Someday, your kids will taunt you with it."

A shadow flashes across his face before he covers it with a smile. "I have dirt on the guys, too."

"Ooh, more gossip. I'll be right back!"

I make him a plate of leftovers, then put two slices of

cherry pie on a plate for our dessert. His eyes grow about three sizes when I hand it to him. Climbing in bed beside him, I flip through the T.V. channels, stopping at one of my favorite Christmas movies.

"Scrooged?" he says.

"I love Bill Murray."

"Me too. Ghostbusters is better."

Lying back beside him, I stack up the pillows so I can see. "Yeah, but it's not a Christmas movie."

He finishes his food, sets the plate on the bedside table, and shakes his head at the plate of pie. "Maybe in a few minutes. Now." He lies beside me, grinning that little boy grin that shows his dimple. "What horrible thing has been imprinted on your brain?"

My head falls to my palm. "Vagsquatch."

"What?"

"My cousin, Chloe, she's a nice girl and everything, but she's a little..."

"Slutty?"

"The C and L in her name should be silent."

Noble bursts out laughing. "That bad?"

I go on to describe the horror I witnessed at dinner and the fact that Denton has been cloistered in her room with her ever since.

"Ha! Perfect! I needed something to give him shit for after today! I fucking love you."

Whoa.

Did I just hear that right?

The wide eyed, cautious expression on Noble's face assures me I did. "I'm sorry, I—."

My voice falls to a whisper. "You're sorry you love me, or you're sorry you said it?"

"No, I'm not sorry for either." He sits up and runs his hands through his hair. I give him a minute to gather his thoughts. His eyes meet mine, shining with sincerity as he says. "I love you, January. I think I loved you before you ever noticed I was alive. I'm not sorry for that. I just...didn't mean to blurt it out when we were talking about hairy twats."

117

A surge of emotion rushes through me. I'm trying not to laugh over his last comment, over the whole situation, really, but I'm also overwhelmed by his confession. And it's time to admit my own.

"When you showed up at the hospital, and I saw you so concerned about me and Mom, those were the first words that went through my brain. Well, you know, after I accidentally beat you up."

A smile creeps across his face, and I brush the hair off his forehead. Bed head looks good on him. "I couldn't believe you came all this way. But it's not just that. I have so much fun with you. I think about you whenever we aren't together. I-I have some issues that just wouldn't allow me to say it first. So, I'm glad you did. Even if we were discussing Chewbacca crotch."

The unsure grin on his face is so adorable, I want to maul him. "Yeah? You love me?"

I drape my leg over his lap, straddling him. "I love you."

"It's about fucking time."

Christmas Day is one of the best I've ever had. Possibly because I have spent the entirety of it in bed with Noble, trying to put the Kama Sutra to shame. Before him, I liked sex, but I could take it or leave it. After all, my hand could usually give me a better ending than a man could. I had no idea what I was missing.

By evening, I finally manage to shower, dress, and leave the room for some food. Mom is being released from the hospital, but Aunt Helen is picking her up. It's a strange feeling, not to be the one solely responsible. I won't be reminding her of her pills, making sure she gets to her appointments, or sitting at the hospital when she has a bad episode.

It's a huge weight off my shoulders, but I also know there are a lot of things I'll miss as well. I'm not sure how I'll deal with living alone, but I'm kind of excited to see.

Denton stands in front of the huge refrigerator, balancing multiple dishes as he roots around. "Hey, Jani, Helen told me to help myself." He turns and sets the dishes on the island. "Do you want some pie?"

"Nah, I'm going to make a couple of turkey sandwiches."

He scoots the platter of turkey across to me. "How is tinkle face?"

"Almost back to normal. You're never going to let that go, are you?"

His grin is infectious. "Would you?"

"Fair point. I'm not sure when we're heading back. I'll check with Cassidy tonight."

"Don't hurry on my account." He gathers up the plates of pie and starts toward the door.

"Don't knock her up!"

"I wrap my monster. Don't worry, I won't cross our bloodlines."

Oh god. I hadn't even thought of that.

My phone beeps with a text from Noble. I figured he must want a drink or something along those lines until I see it's a picture message. My service isn't great here, and the picture takes a moment to load, so I lay the phone on the counter while I slather mayo on bread and add some turkey and lettuce.

The kitchen door pops open and Mom walks through with Aunt Helen right behind her. "Jani! Merry Christmas!" Mom exclaims. They're both beaming from ear to ear.

"Merry Christmas. It's good to see you so chipper."

"I'm glad to be home."

Home. This is her home now.

She glances at my phone that's glowing on the counter. Her gaze also draws Aunt Helen's attention, who peeks over her shoulder. It doesn't even register in my mind they're looking at the picture Noble sent me until Aunt Helen chokes on a laugh, and Mom announces, "Not bad. Leans a little to the left. I'm glad to see you're having a good day. Helen and I are going to work on her new puzzle."

They leave the room like hell is chasing them, their

laughter following them down the long hall.

I snatch the phone up to see a crystal clear, up close and personal picture of Noble's erect cock.

Damn it all.

I'm going to kill him.

I shove the phone in my pocket and haul our food and drinks back to our room. Any thoughts of talking to Helen about getting Mom's things have been put on hold. No way am I facing her now.

"Seriously? You sent me a dick pic from the next room?"

Noble is stretched out on the bed, a Chesire Cat smile on his face. "I thought you might miss him."

"Well, Mom and Aunt Helen didn't miss him."

The covers fly off as he shoots bolt upright. "What? Why did you let them see your phone?"

"I laid it on the counter. I didn't expect it to be a phone boner! How are you even hard? We've been at it all day!"

"That's your fault. All I have to do is picture you, and that ass."

"Well, they saw it."

He takes his plate from me. "What did they say?"

"They laughed and left." I climb onto the bed beside him.

"Laughed? Psh. Some women can't handle it. That's why I named it Truth."

Blinking, I stare at him, trying to make sense of that statement.

He chuckles and grabs at his sweat pant clad crotch. "You want the truth? You can't handle the truth!"

"Oh god. You're such a dork sometimes."

He plants a quick kiss on my cheek. "But you love me. So, you're stuck. Besides, you know you touch yourself when you think about me."

"I facepalm. Does that count?"

"With you, sweetheart. I'll take what I can get."

My phone beeps again, and I give him a look. He holds up his palms. "Not me, I swear."

"It's Cass. They want to meet for breakfast in the morning."

"Are we flying back tomorrow?"

"I don't know. Guess we'll ask them then."

Noble sets our now empty plates aside. "In the meantime…"

By the next morning, my vagina hates me and is in full revolt. "Get away from me, you sex fiend," I groan, when Noble's arms find their way around me again, pulling me close.

His chuckle is warm in my ear. "I'll behave myself. We have to meet Cass in an hour. You'd better get up."

"I can't. I have a crippled snooch."

"Do you want me to lick it better?"

"No, no touching for at least twenty-four hours. I'm trying to get up the courage to pee."

He slaps me on the ass. "Well, get moving. I'm starving."

"You slap my ass a lot," I remark, rolling out of bed.

"What can I say? It's slappable."

"I'm going to take that as a compliment."

"You should."

An hour later, we're cleaned up and seated on a patio under a copse of palm trees. Cassidy and Wyatt walk in, and I know something is up since Cass's face is all smile.

"Hey guys, how was your holiday?" she asks.

The sideways glance I give Noble makes Cass laugh. "The same as ours then. So, we have a little favor to ask."

"Name it," Noble says. After flying him and Denton here, I'm sure he's hoping for a chance to return a favor.

Cass smiles at Wyatt, and he returns it, nodding. "We're going to get married while we're here. Like, this evening."

What?

"But…how did you arrange…?"

They laugh at our stunned faces. "It wasn't hard. We found an officiant to do the ceremony. We pick up the license after we leave here, and we don't need a venue when we're surrounded by beautiful beaches."

I get to my feet and hug Cass. "I'm so happy for you! What do you need from us?"

"We want you to be witnesses, and I need to find a dress. Just something light and pretty."

Noble shakes Wyatt's hand. "Congratulations, man. I'd be honored."

"My cousin, Chloe, is a photography student. I'm sure she'd be happy to take pictures if you'd like. Unless you want to hire a professional."

Cass beams. "We don't really have time to find anyone, so that would be perfect." She squeezes Wyatt's arm as she continues. "Wyatt needs to find a suit, so I was thinking maybe he and Noble could go shopping, and we could do the same. We'll find you a dress too." She turns to Wyatt. "And we should include Denton. You guys go get all pretty and we'll handle the rest," she gushes. "Oh, wait! A cake. The hotel manager told me there's a bakery on Main Street that should have something pre-made, so you can pick that up."

When no one moves, she huffs, "Well, what are you waiting for? We don't have much time. Let's go!"

Noble and Wyatt exchange a look, trying not to smile.

"Okay, I'll handle Bridezilla here. Why don't we meet at the hotel around two?" I suggest.

Noble leans over and drops a kiss on my ear before we part, murmuring, "Bye, babe. Try not to walk so funny."

Bastard.

Chapter Nine

Noble

I've somehow been roped into an impromptu wedding, but it's the least I can do after what Cassidy and Wyatt have done for us. Wyatt and I head back to the house to pick up Denton, who is more than happy to go along as well. He seems a bit relieved to distance himself from Chloe, who practically humps his leg as we're leaving.

Wyatt laughs as we climb into his rental car. "That didn't take long. You might want to be careful. She's got those crazy, *I might follow you back to the mainland* eyes."

Denton slumps in his seat. "She's a monster in bed, but damn, way too clingy. I'm glad I live far away."

"If the pussy is good, just enjoy it while we're here," Wyatt advises. "It'll only be another day or so."

"So, is it?" I ask, turning to regard him in the back seat.

"Good pussy? Oh yeah." He fidgets a bit, looking out the window.

They both look at me when a snort of laughter springs forth.

"What am I missing?" Wyatt asks.

"Nothing. Denton's spent the last couple of days taming the wild buffalo."

Denton's gaze jerks to mine. "How the hell do you know that?"

"Jani got an eyeful at dinner the other night. She said it was full woolly mammoth land."

Groaning, Denton covers his eyes, and leans back.

Wyatt chuckles. "So she's—"

"All snatchural," I interrupt. "It's not like there's anything wrong with that. I mean, I prefer not to have to use a sickle to find the wet spot, but to each their own."

"Hey." Wyatt speaks up, amusement in his voice. "Don't let him give you shit, Denton. We've all come face to face with a bikini spider a time or two. You still got to own that shit like a man."

The conversation ends when Wyatt parks in front of a men's clothing store. Shopping isn't high on any of our lists, but once we explain to the sales lady what's going on and what we need, it's relatively painless. We walk out with our new suits less than an hour later.

The next stop is the bakery where Wyatt picks up a fancy white cake. It's not really meant to be a wedding cake, but who cares? You can't go wrong with cake and this is all last minute, anyway. With all our errands run, we head back to the hotel to wait on the girls.

Wyatt's hotel suite is spacious and steeped in luxury I'll never know in my lifetime. Denton and I take a seat at the shiny wooden table while Wyatt checks his phone. "They decided to get their hair done as well, so they'll be a while."

I grin at Wyatt as he sits across from us. "So, are you terrified yet? Ready to run into the ocean?"

"Nah, Cass is it for me. I want to get that ring on her finger, make sure she knows it." He reaches back to a mini fridge behind him and passes us a beer.

Denton pops his open, takes a swig, then turns his attention to me. "How are things going with Jani?"

"I may have blurted out an I love you. Right after showing my dick to her mother and her aunt."

They both pause before breaking into laughter. "What the

fuck have you been doing?" Denton asks.

"Okay, the dick reveal wasn't my fault. I sent her a picture, and she left her phone open. Her family is just too damn nosy. The I love you..." I run my hands through my hair. "It just popped out."

"Like in the middle of sex? Because that doesn't count," Denton informs me.

"Nope, we were just talking."

"Did you mean it?"

Wyatt leans forward, his elbows on the table. "Of course he did. That shit doesn't just pop out for no reason." He nods at me. "I know how it is. It kind of builds up until it escapes on its own."

"Exactly."

Wyatt finishes his beer. "So, did she respond?"

"Yeah, she said it back. We're good."

The smile on Denton's face is taunting. "So, we could easily make this a double wedding today."

"Ha! You can fuck right off with that. We're too young. I've got two years of school left."

Denton slaps me on the arm. "I'm just fucking with you. Jani's a great girl. I'm happy for you."

"So, how far along is Cass?" I ask.

Wyatt's jaw plummets, and he lets out a bark of laughter. "How the fuck did you know?"

"Dude, come on. Impromptu wedding because you're in Hawaii? You two can fly wherever you want anytime."

Wyatt shakes his head. "She's only about six weeks. And don't tell Jani. We aren't announcing anything for a while."

"Congrats, man," Denton tells him. "Kids are great." He pokes me in the arm. "You're next."

Forcing a smile, I shove him. "No way. I like having my time and money all to myself." It's what I've always told myself. I found out at eighteen that I'm sterile. When I was trying to come up with money for college, I went to a sperm bank to sell my swimmers, and they called me that night to tell me. At eighteen, my first thought was that it was probably a good thing, that I wouldn't be able to accidentally get a woman pregnant. It's easier to tell people I don't want kids than I can't have them, and spare myself that look of pity. I don't really brood on it, I mean, at my age, I'm not exactly dying to be a father. I still haven't found a way to tell my mother, though.

"It's a little earlier than we planned," Wyatt confesses. "But I'm looking forward to being a dad."

The rest of the afternoon marches by, and the evening finds me standing on a beach with my friends, watching two of them marry.

Cassidy and Wyatt stand together, reading their vows to one another, but I don't really hear them. I can't take my eyes off of Jani. She's so beautiful. I've never seen her in a dress since she's more of a jeans and sweater type of girl.

The airy, flowing, pale yellow dress she wears flutters in the salty breeze, and she smiles at me from her place on the other side of Cassidy. A white and yellow ribbon holds back her dark hair, showing the long line of her neck. She catches me looking at her and glances toward the happy couple, widening her eyes, then looks back at me, her expression clearly conveying her thoughts. It's like we can talk without saying a word.

It's surreal to watch the people you care about, the same people you learned to swim the turbulent waters of adulthood with, take such a huge step. It puts our lives in perspective, how far we've come from being clueless kids learning to pay bills and stumbling our way through first dates to making huge life decisions.

A small ball of panic settles into my stomach. It's like all the expectations of the future are attacking me at once. I have to finish school, and while I have a scholarship for the next two years, I have a sizable student loan to pay off for the last four. I have a new job, but it's also pretty temporary. I don't have to look far to find the horror stories of graduates struggling to find work in their field.

Jani turns back toward the happy couple, and her eyes well up as she watches them kiss. The panic ball in my stomach swells a bit more. She loves me. And she knows I love her. How long before marriage is added to the pile of expectations already balancing on my back? And surely, she'll want kids; a family. I was so bent on getting her to want me like I wanted her, I didn't think about the future at all.

It's too much.

The officiant pronounces them man and wife, and I smile and clap along with Denton, Helen, Aubrey, and Brinna, while Chloe snaps pictures. Cass and Wyatt radiate happiness. I can't let my sudden realization ruin their moment.

Wyatt shakes my hand while Cass and Jani hug. "Thanks for being here," Wyatt says. He flashes a sideways look at Jani before adding. "I'll be happy to return the favor when it's your turn."

His words reach her ears as well and she just smiles at me. Expectations.

I'm drowning in them.

I manage to keep my cool through the rest of the night and I'm relieved when we climb on the plane to head back home to Indiana. I have a new job to start, and new classes I haven't done the required reading for. This little jaunt into paradise has been fun, but real life awaits.

Bigger and more intimidating than ever.

My phone beeps with a message from Jani.

Jani: Dinner tonight?

My chest thumps against my ribs. I want to see her. I really do. I've been busy with schoolwork and my new job since we got home over a week ago, but that isn't the reason I haven't been spending time with her. Seeing Cass and Wyatt tie the knot made me realize I need a plan for my life. I've been chugging along, trying my best, but I've never really stepped back and thought about what I want long term.

My first thought is her. I want Jani forever, but I'm not ready to be responsible for other people's lives. She loves me. She'll want to move in together which will lead to marriage and buying a house. I don't even know where I want to live after school is over, or what career I'll end up in. And kids. She's never had much family, just her mother, and if she stays with me, she never will.

That's what I tell myself.

That's how I justify ghosting the woman I've chased for years. The woman I love and think about every fucking second.

My hand trembles as I type a reply to her message.

Me: Sorry, busy studying.

The three dots blink for a bit as if she's typing a message back, but then disappear. I lie back on my bed, staring at the ceiling until I hear another beep a few minutes later.

Jani: Are you avoiding me? Are you pissed about something?

Fuck. I'm such a coward. I have to just come out with it before I change my mind.

Me: You didn't do anything. I just need some space. I think we should take a break.

My heart is being yanked out through my navel, and I'd rather be stung in the face by a jellyfish again than send the message, but I do. This time her response is much faster.

Jani: Go fuck yourself.

I spend the rest of the night tossing and turning, thinking about her all alone in her apartment right down the street. Her front door is closed when I drive past on my way to work the next morning, and I wonder if she's sleeping. Is she thinking about me?

Is she hurting and missing me or planning my violent death?

Ed, the video editor waves from his booth when I walk in the studio to begin my second week of work. This job is definitely better than my last, but it's not what I expected. They chose me for my major in meteorology, but all I'm ever asked to do is run errands for the other employees. I don't know why I need a background in climate science to make coffee and answer phones.

"Noble!" Ed calls, popping out of his booth and making his way over to me. "Who farted on your Pop-Tart this morning?"

"What?" My mind was elsewhere, as usual. Ed is a weird guy, but I like weird people. They're usually the most fun. Until they start talking about farting on a Pop-Tart.

"You look like you lost your best friend. Is everything okay?"

No, everything is shit, and I don't know how it got to this point. "I'm fine. Cream and no sugar, right?" I mumble, starting down the hall to the break room.

"Stop." He grabs my arm. "I've already got a coffee. Harrison is looking for you."

Great. If the producer wants to talk to a lowly student intern, I can't imagine it's great news. Maybe I'm not cut out to be their coffee gopher after all. "Great, thanks."

Harrison's office door is ajar, and I barely have the time to tap on it before he barks, "Come in."

I've only met Harrison once when the assistant producer was showing me around. He's almost as wide as the doorway and if any of it is muscle, it's well hidden by years of donuts and deep-fried Twinkies. He's been trying to slim down, judging by the chocolate weight loss shakes in the break room fridge, but someone should tell him they don't work if you add chocolate syrup. Yeah, walked in on that one during my second day.

"You wanted to see me?"

"Yes." He doesn't even glance up from the paperwork on his desk. "The Science Dude just cancelled last minute, and the kids are due here shortly. You need to get ready to take his place."

What? He can't be suggesting...

"The supplies are under the weather desk. Set up in room

three."

"I-you want me to do a science experiment with a bunch of kids?"

His eyebrows rise, and he looks up at me. "Science is your field, is it not?"

"Well, yeah, but." A horrific thought strikes me. "Wait. You don't mean like, live, on air?"

Sighing, he shuffles some papers around. "Well, I didn't mean for my own personal entertainment. I realize you haven't been on air before, but there's nothing to it. You have an hour to prepare. Just engage the children, let them do the experiment, and smile."

His tone makes it clear I'm dismissed, so I wander back down the hall. Angie, the assistant producer sees me and bursts out laughing.

"Noble, you look like you're going to pass out. It isn't that bad. Come on. I'll show you."

She leads me to room three where a three-foot-tall volcano waits. "The Science Dude sent this."

The paper she hands me has simple step by step instructions of how to make the volcano "erupt" using clear soda, food coloring, and Mentos candy.

"I made a volcano in elementary school once, but used hydrogen peroxide and baking soda," I mumble, reading the instructions. It seems pretty straightforward, but something tells me doing this with a bunch of kids and a camera pointed at me won't be simple. I used to want to be a weatherman, but right now I can't remember why I ever thought it was a good idea.

"Same basic principle, I suppose," Angie says.

"Well, not really. It's not a chemical reaction, but a physical one called nucleation. The gas bubbles adhere to the tiny craters in the candy and—"

Angie's bored off her tits expression cuts my explanation short, and I run a hand through my hair. "Yeah, mix the ingredients and the volcano goes boom. Same deal. How many kids are going to be here?"

"Fifteen, but only two have been chosen to help you and

ask questions. The others know to keep quiet until the camera is off. Then you can answer any additional questions. The whole segment is only five minutes, and I'll give you the signal when you need to wrap it up. I sent Heather to get the soda. She should be back any time. Any questions?"

"Can they keep the camera above my waist in case I wet myself?"

Angie laughs and rolls her eyes. "You'll be fine."

I don't feel fine. I spend the next hour trying to give myself a pep talk, and rereading the instructions left by the Science Dude. It is very simple, although he's tried to dress it up a bit for the kids. Instead of just dumping the dyed soda into the top along with a few candies, he's rigged up a little system.

An empty container sits inside the shell of the volcano, waiting to be filled with soda. The elongated neck of the container should concentrate the flow and make it more forceful. A small makeshift drawer is cut into the side of the plaster so the candy can be introduced. It slides down a chute into the container and voila, it's a sticky fountain of lava. The entire thing rests in a square, flat container meant to catch the runoff, but I imagine it's still going to be a bit of a mess.

"Here you go," Heather, the only other intern says, placing three two-liter bottles of soda on the table beside me. "They didn't have regular, so I had to get diet."

"It's clear. That should be all that matters." I mumble a quick thank you and proceed to add red food coloring to the bottles. It takes quite a bit to turn the soda red instead of pink, but I have enough. A faint fizzing can be heard as I carefully fill up the container, careful not to drip any "lava" on the outer shell.

They went a little overboard on the candy since the directions call for adding seven or eight candies to the chute, and there's a bowl with thirty or more waiting to be used.

The sound of many sneakers on tile reaches my ears, along with the murmur of little voices and the shushing of what I assume is a teacher. Oh god.

The kids are here.

I'm not that great with kids, not because I don't like them, but because I've never really been around them. I don't know how to talk to kids, or at what level they can understand at different ages. I'm an only child so I've never had nieces or nephews around, and all my cousins were older than me.

A smiling face appears at the door. "Are you ready for us?" the young woman asks.

No. So much no.

"Come on in," I call, planting a smile on my face faker than those *grow a bigger dick* pill ads you see on the porn sites. Not that I've ever tried one. My twenty-first digit is quite satisfactory.

She's followed by a line of kids around six or seven years old. Wide eyes pan around the room, taking in all of the equipment.

"Hey kids!" I call out. Great, I sound like Krusty the damn Clown. "Are you ready to help me make a huge mess?"

Giggles and nods from the shyer kids are accompanied by louder exclamations of "Yes!" from the others.

Angie returns and shows them each where they need to stand for the camera to make sure they're all in the shot, then steps back behind the cameraman. Angie explained earlier that they won't count down to when we go live, because kids tend to be more interested in waving or making faces at the camera than paying attention once they know we're live.

I've pretty much memorized the notes the Science Dude left, so I set them aside and paste on a big smile when the cameraman points at me, letting me know we're live.

Okay, I can do this. It's not like this is national television. It's a local station in a rural area. There's probably like two farmers and a few bored housewives watching while painting their toenails.

"Okay," I begin. "Today we're going to talk about physical and chemical reactions and some of the fun ways we can see them in everyday life."

That's all I get out before I'm interrupted by a little boy with a buzzed haircut. "You aren't the Science Dude!"

"Well, no, I'm not. The Science Dude wasn't feeling too well today, so I'm—"

"The Science Dude is black. You're not black," the same kid announces. When this is over, I'm going to wedgie him. Seriously. I'm not too proud to do it. Maybe even an atomic one.

Ignoring him, I continue, "Right, as I was saying, the Science Dude wasn't feeling well, so I'm going to show you how cool this is instead."

"Yeah," another brat interjects. "The Science Dude has cool hair and he's black. Why aren't you?"

What the? Why am I not black? How do I answer that? The clock is ticking and this whole thing has turned into a shit show.

"Because my parents aren't black." It's the simplest explanation I can give.

Their teacher gives the group a severe look which seems to work, at least for the moment, and I'm able to quickly run through the differences between the types of reactions. The two kids who have been chosen to help step up, and I explain what we're going to do.

"Okay, you can drop the candies into the chute," I offer, speaking to a little girl in a white dress. "Just count out eight and…"

Too late.

She dumps the whole bowl into the drawer, and I'm pretty sure my job goes rattling down the chute along with them. The result is instantaneous.

A gush of bright red soda erupts, almost reaching the rafters, and rains down on everything. There isn't one kid, camera, or speck of floor that isn't doused in the sticky liquid. I'm standing in the middle of a bloodbath surrounded by crying, giggling, squealing kids.

If that isn't enough of a kick in the taint, my foot slides on the slick floor. I swear, I didn't mean to take a kid down with me, but, you know, when you start to fall, you grab for anything, and the little girl who caused all this was right there.

In a stunning show of grace, I fall on my ass, pulling her down with me. She's not hurt, but the white dress will never be the same.

There's nothing left to lose now. Still sitting on the floor, I face the camera and say, "So, yeah, a prime example of a physical reaction. If you try this at home, I suggest a poncho, and far fewer children. Back to you, Lee."

Lee, along with the other anchor, are laughing too hard to pick it up, so they toss it to Dean, the weather guy, who manages to give the forecast, though it's peppered with quite a few chuckles.

The teacher apologizes profusely while Angie and Heather lead the kids down the hall to the restroom to clean up. Yeah, good luck with that. Even a shower may not get it all out, judging by how much coloring I put in.

Defeated, I sit and lean against the wall, a red puddle surrounding me. I'm wondering if the meat department at the supercenter might take me back when Harrison pokes his head in. His husky, smoke choked laugh bounces off the walls.

"Damn boy, I thought the others had to be exaggerating."

"Afraid not." Just fire me and get it over with.

"I'll get janitorial in. You may want to make yourself scarce. They won't be happy with you. Take the rest of the day off. I got five bucks says you won't get all that dye off."

My eyebrows jump up and the words fall out of my mouth. "I still have a job?"

Harrison smiles at me. "Why do you think I handed this off to an intern? Fifteen kids and a volcano? No way that was going to run smoothly. I didn't expect it to look like a scene from Carrie, but still, no one else would've done it."

I drag myself to my feet. "Yeah, thanks for that."

"Welcome to the team, kid." With that, he leaves me to slosh my way out of the building.

I will say one thing for the shitty day I've had; it's the first time since I dropped Jani off that I haven't thought about her. Epic failures are good for a distraction.

When I push through the studio's back door, I realize my day isn't over. Cassidy stands there, her arms crossed, the angry expression on her face evolving into confusion. "What the hell happened to you?"

Shivering, I stalk toward my car and pull my emergency

blanket out of the trunk. The same one Jani used after I took her magnet fishing. God, I miss her. "It's a long story and I'm not in the mood to tell it right now, Cass."

"I don't give a shit what you're in the mood for."

Doubled over, the blanket should at least protect my car seat from looking like the scene of a massacre.

Cass grabs my arm, pulling me away from the car. "What happened with Jani? She said you stopped calling, then broke up over a text!"

"Then you know what happened," I mumble, trying to take a step back.

"Don't give me that smart ass shit. I'm better at it than you."

Sighing, I reach in and turn the heat on full blast, then gesture to the passenger seat. "Can you at least ream me out where it's warm?"

I'm grateful my car warms up quickly as the hot air washes over me, taking my shivering with it.

Cass glares at me. "Okay. Explain. Because the look on your face when I mentioned her name tells me you're hurting just as much as she is."

My chest tightens at the thought of her suffering because of me. I lean my head back and the words pour out. "It's too much. School, my job, buying a house, kids. I can't do it. Not yet."

"Jani wants a house and kids?" Cassidy exclaims with a blink, her voice incredulous.

"Don't all women? And I can't do that. I love being with Jani. I love *her*. But I feel like I'm trapped in a box with the air slowly being sucked out."

Cassidy looks at me like I might be brain dead. "Just to clarify, Jani has never mentioned this house and kids you're so freaked out about?"

"Well, no, but it's not just that. I have two years of school left and no idea what I'm going to do after. I might never be ready for all that. And Jani deserves those things. She deserves the best."

Cass sighs and places her hand on my arm, giving it a gentle squeeze. "Noble, your heart's in the right place, but your head is up your ass."

Stunned, I gape at her until she continues.

"I don't know why you suddenly think that—" Her eyes widen as she interrupts herself. "Wait, is this because Wyatt and I got married?"

I shrug and stare out my window. "Married, own your own home, baby on the way. Jani was so happy for you. I want her to have that too."

Her voice is patient, like she's talking to a child. "We did those things because we decided together that we were ready. The same way you and Jani should decide the direction of your relationship together. I get that you're stressed because of everything on your shoulders now, but that's life. Suck it up. Your life is no different than it was when you and Jani started dating. You're worrying over nothing. Did it ever occur to you to ask her what she wants instead of assuming?"

Hmm. She may have a point. Is it all in my head? Did I just stress out and panic for no reason?

"I can't have kids. Ever. My guys don't swim."

The words come out a little easier than I thought they would, considering I've never told another person.

Cassidy's face fills with sympathy. "I'm sorry. That really sucks. But there are always alternatives, and right now, it's just not an issue."

I shift in my seat, and look her in the eye. "Do you think she'll take me back?"

"She loves you." Her gaze sweeps over me. "But maybe go home and shower before you try. You look like a giant tampon."

As she climbs out of my car, she bends to add, "Tell her what you told me. All of it. You aren't the only one who feels adulthood like a leash around your neck."

"Thanks, Cass."

"Anytime, dumbass."

Chapter Ten

A reality show blares from the television while I eat my weight in chocolate truffle ice cream. See, this is why I don't do relationships. I know better. Years of watching Mom brood and suffer over the guy who didn't love her should've taught me better, but here I am, feeling stupid with a broken heart.

Was it because I said I loved him? I mean, he said it first. True, he blurted it out while he was laughing, so maybe that didn't count. Me saying it back most likely scared him away. It's probably for the best, anyway. The end was inevitable, and I would've only grown more attached.

I knew something wasn't right a few days after we returned from Hawaii. Noble went from spending every available second with me to making excuses about schoolwork. My mind had been dreaming up all the dirty stuff we could do now that I had the apartment all to myself, and instead, I'm sitting here alone, with reality shows on T.V. because it makes me miss Mom a little less.

Last night, I decided I was tired of the games and texted him, asking if he was angry at me, or what was going on. I don't know what I expected, but him responding with needing a break wasn't it. A break. I should break him like a fucking Kit Kat bar, but I don't want to give him the satisfaction of knowing he's hurt me.

I've kept busy by packing up all of Mom's things for the shipping company that's coming by today. I can only imagine what Aunt Helen paid to send all these boxes to Hawaii.

My phone pings with a message from an unfamiliar number.

Hello, I saw your ad about the ring found in White River. My name is Gerald Harper, and I believe it belongs to me. The inscription should read, *To my dear Maeetta, the loveliest woman.*

A smile jumps onto my face for the first time in a week. My life may suck at the moment, but it looks like I'll be able to make someone's day.

Me: Yes, it's your ring. I'd be happy to return it to you.
Him: I work at the coffee shop next door to the university every day from nine to five. Would you mind bringing it by?

It's only eight a.m. now. Yes, I was eating ice cream for breakfast. Don't judge me.

Me: I'll stop by today.
Him: Thank you.

I can't wait to hear the story behind the ring. Maybe it will renew my faith in love and relationships. I've built a little narrative in my head of a cute older couple, out fishing on the river, when his wife loses the ring. She's distraught for days, even though he buys her a new one. There's no replacing the sentiment of the original ring. I imagine him bringing it to her, and her squeal of happiness. Noble was amused when I told him the story, but what the hell does he know? I want to believe that. I need to believe there are happy endings out there, at least for some people.

The ice cream goes back into the freezer, and I take a quick shower. I'm running the flat iron through my hair when the shipping company arrives. By the time they have all Mom's stuff loaded, I'm ready to go.

The little coffee shop is bustling with college students, laughing and chatting over their phones and laptops. A corner table with five girls erupts into giggles as I walk in. Ugh. I'm suddenly happy I didn't do the college thing. I'd still like to take some business classes, but living in a dorm surrounded by these women would send me off the nearest bridge.

An older man works the counter. He hands a young man a cup, then smiles at me. "What can I get you?"

"Mr. Harper? I'm January. I found your wife's ring."

"Right, yeah, thanks for coming down here." He turns and yells for another employee to relieve him, then leads me to an empty table.

"I can't believe you found it. After seeing your ad, I Googled magnet fishing. I hadn't ever heard of it, but it looks interesting. It's sure going to save me a lot of money."

His statement is confusing, but I don't bother to ask him to clarify. Taking the ring from my pocket, I hand it to him. "It needs cleaning, as you can see, but it should be restorable." A pang shoots through me as I show him my wrist—more specifically the silver bracelet hanging from it. "We found this at the same time and it was in far worse shape."

"Well, turn me upside down and paint me blue. How about that?" He marvels at the difference in the thickly tarnished ring and the shiny bracelet.

"Do you mind telling me how it was lost? I'm sure it's an interesting story."

His face darkens. "Yeah, damn movie of the week," he scoffs. "My wife and I were married for almost twenty-one years. I bought her this ring on our twentieth wedding anniversary. That was nearly a year before I found out she was screwing the neighbor and had been for ten years. The topper was discovering my youngest son wasn't mine."

The swell of hope I felt dissipates like dew in the sunshine.

"Oh, I'm so sorry. I-did she throw the ring away?"

"No, I did. It was stupid, but I was angry. Then she sued for the ring in the divorce and won. Since I couldn't produce it, they've been after me for the money." A devious smile inches across his face, drawing lines around his mouth. "Now, she can have it back, just like it is."

So, theory confirmed. Love is bullshit.

Getting to my feet, I slip my coat on. "Great. Well, I'm glad I could help you out."

"Let me get you some breakfast," he offers. "It's the least I can do."

"No thank you. I've already eaten."

"A coffee then."

The ice cream I ate is bubbling on my stomach. "Thanks, but I have to run."

I make it to the door before one of the giggling girls calls out, "Aren't you dating PP?"

The whole table stares at me like I have toilet paper hanging out of my pants or something. "PP?" I repeat, taking a few steps to their table.

The group laughs, and one of the girls speaks up, "You're seeing Noble Bradley, right?"

"Ah, well, something like that."

They all nod knowingly. "See, he's taken. I told you," a blonde says to the girl next to her.

There's no way I'm telling them he's available. "Why did you call him PP?"

They all giggle again, and I want to permanently cauterize their vocal cords by the time one of them speaks up. "Sorry, that's what he's known by at school." She drops her voice. "You know, because of his porn penis."

Lord help me.

My heart gallops as I ask. "Have any of you actually seen it?"

Their faces fall. "No, so you have to tell us. Is it true? They say it's like twelve inches long," the blonde says, awe ringing in her voice.

Oh, this is just too perfect of an opportunity.

I flip my hair over my shoulder and lean in. "You shouldn't believe everything you hear, girls. Twelve inches? It's four tops, although, it does sometimes smell like a foot."

I choke back a laugh as their mouths all fall open in a perfect O.

"You're kidding," the blonde breathes.

"Nope, hung like a baby carrot, poor guy. I don't know where that rumor got started. He's a nice guy, though, and there are more important things, you know? I've got to run. Have a good day, girls."

They're leaned in with their heads together, whispering furiously before I make it out the door.

That felt better than it should have. It almost makes up for the disappointment of finding out the ring was attached to a depressing divorce story.

I have just enough time to swing by my apartment and grab my tablet before heading to work. I know it's going to be a long day, so I definitely need a distraction. Love in real life may be a myth, but my book boyfriends never let me down.

Work drags by. Don't get me wrong. I absolutely love my job at Scarlet Toys, but a gloom has settled over me I can't seem to shake.

Fucking Noble.

Stupid, cute asshole.

I hope he trips and squishes his porn penis into a little Vienna sausage.

My only real entertainment of the day comes when Clarence pokes his head into the office. "Hey, Jani, there's a woman out here insisting on talking to a manager."

Great. The last time this happened it was a young woman wanting advice on how to remove a small dildo that "got sucked into" her ass. I manage a sex store. I'm not a doctor. I'm sure the fact her ass left the room two minutes after she did contributed to the issue, but, you know, I had to be nice and professional. Sometimes it's a struggle.

A lady stands at the counter, a giant purse tucked under

her arm, receipt in hand. Now, our policy—and yeah, we actually need one—is no returns that have been opened unless they are defective and unused.

The whopper of a vibrator she's waving around definitely doesn't qualify.

"Hi, I'm the manager. How can I help you?"

She purses her lips. "As I've been trying to explain to your employees, this is not what I paid for. The package says it offers intense vibrations. This thing barely buzzes." I take a step back at the sight of the obviously used and not well cleaned vibe. She flips it on and it nearly rattles out of her hand. If that's not strong enough, I don't know what the hell would be. But I'm also not going to argue this. It's gross, and I just want her gone.

"I'm sorry about that." I recognize the item and grab another off the shelf to check the price.

"Clarence, please refund her sixty-seven dollars and ninety-nine cents."

"Thank you." She tries to hand it to me, and I have to swallow back a vurp. You know, a vomit burp.

"You can keep it. Thanks for shopping with us."

Satisfied, she takes her money and exits.

Clarence and Henry burst out laughing, and I shudder. "So gross."

"She shouldn't get a refund," Henry says. "It's not our fault she needs a toy with a twelve-volt battery and pull start like a lawnmower."

"I'm not about to argue over a crusty vibrator. I'll take the loss."

The front door dings, and I look up to see Cassidy grinning at me.

"Hey, boss lady!" Clarence exclaims, hugging her.

"I'm not the boss lady anymore." She laughs and nods at me. "Jani isn't being too tough on you, is she?"

"Nah, she's a peach. You just missed a woman trying to return a dirty vibrator, though."

"I'll try to get over the disappointment." She grabs my arm and drags me back to the office.

"What? Did Wyatt do something? I'll clip his nuts off like a dog. I'm in that state of mind."

"No." She takes a seat on my desk, her legs swinging in front of her. "I have news. News I thought Wyatt and I agreed not to share for a while, but apparently Noble knows, so you should too."

My heart jumps to life at the sound of his name, and I resist asking a dozen questions. Like when did you talk to him? How is he doing? Is he seeing someone else? Did you know they call him porn penis at school?

Instead, I stamp a smile on my face. "Okay, shoot."

"I'm pregnant."

It takes a second for me to absorb her words. "No shit?"

Her laughter spills into the hallway. "Yeah, no shit. I wanted to wait until the second trimester to tell anyone, but it's been killing me."

"Congratulations! I'm so happy for you! Oh my god, you and Wyatt are going to make the cutest babies ever!"

We laugh, and I hug her hard, nearly knocking her off the desk. I know how much Cassidy wanted a family. This is her dream come true.

When we calm down, she looks me in the eye and asks, "Do you want kids someday?"

I chew my lip and shake my head. "I know it probably makes me sound like a selfish bitch, but no, I don't think I do. I mean, it's great for you and Wyatt, and I couldn't be happier for you, but I like my freedom. I want to be able to sleep in on my days off and do what I want without worrying about the extra responsibility."

Cassidy smiles at me. "It's not selfish at all. It would be more selfish to have kids because it's expected when it isn't what you want. You only get one life, so live it the way that will make you happiest, because really, isn't that the whole point of living?"

Nudging her leg with my foot, I grin back at her. "Those hormones have turned you all philosophical already."

"It's put things in perspective. Which is why I want to talk to you about Noble. I think you should give him another chance."

Where the hell did that come from?

"I'm not even sure where to start on this one," I laugh, getting to my feet. "First of all, he broke it off with me, not the other way around, and he hasn't tried to contact me since."

"I know. Now, don't get pissed, but I may have confronted him."

Damn it. I would've done the same thing for her, but still.

"You confronted him? When?"

"A few minutes ago. At his work."

I pace the small office like a trapped moth. "You went to his job to yell at him?"

"Yes, but I didn't yell. I calmly talked to him. He's really hurting too."

"I doubt that. It was his decision."

She hops off the desk. "I know. He fucked up. I don't want to get into details because it's his place to tell you, not mine, but it really had nothing to do with you, Jani. It's all about his own insecurities."

She steps forward and puts her hands on my shoulders. "I'm not taking his side or condoning his bullshit. You know that, right?"

"Yeah." I know better than that. Cass has always had my back.

"Just listen to him when he comes crawling back. Let him explain. Will you do that? You guys are just too good together, and I know how happy you've been. I'd hate to see you throw away a good thing because he got cold feet."

"I'll listen to him, but I can't promise I won't kill him after."

She gives me a hug. "Then call me and we'll dispose of the body."

After talking with Cass, I expect Noble to show up at my place, but I didn't expect him to be a dark shade of pink. His face, neck, hands, and wrists, every bit of skin I can see looks like it's been dipped in Pepto-Bismol.

It broke the ice on an uncomfortable, angsty moment, at least. "What the hell happened to you?" I exclaim.

"It's a long story. Can I come in? Please?"

I step back, letting him inside. His scent wafts behind him and my heart tightens. I've missed him so much. Asshole.

He fidgets uncomfortably, his hands shoved in the pockets of his hoodie. "January, I'm so sorry. I made a huge mistake."

"By dating me or breaking up with me?" I ask, sitting on the couch. If he thinks I'm going to make this easy, and run back into his arms just because he apologizes, he'd better think again. I want to know why.

"I would never describe our relationship as a mistake." He paces the room until I grab his arm.

"Sit down. You're making me nervous."

"Sorry." He sits beside me on the couch.

"Look, I've had a long day and by the looks of you, yours wasn't much better so let's skip the bullshit, okay? Why are you here?"

"I want you back. I know I screwed up, and I'm so sorry. I just…freaked out when I saw Wyatt and Cass getting married. Everything just sort of piled onto me and I felt…I don't know. Overwhelmed."

His blue eyes are filled with sincerity, but I really don't know what he's talking about. "I don't understand."

He rubs the back of his neck. "I guess I'm stressed. School, a new job—which isn't going well, as you can tell." He gestures to his pink skin.

"And I added to your stress?" I clarify, feeling anger beginning to build.

"No. Shit, I'm not explaining this very well. Being with you was the opposite of stressful. I love spending time with you. It was all the things I thought being in love meant, the expectations of marriage, buying a house, having a baby. I suddenly felt like an adult and I'm not prepared to be one. Fuck, I don't feel any different than I did at eighteen."

Is he insane?

"Whoa. Back the hell up. What are you talking about? Noble, I've never asked you for anything. Not one single thing. I've never even mentioned marriage. I mean, we were together for about five minutes. And kids? Are you fucking insane? You think I want kids? What's wrong with you?"

His laugh is bitter. "I wish I knew. I saw Cassidy getting all the things she's ever wanted, and all I could think was how much you deserve those things. And I can't give them to you." His eyes are filled with pain when he looks at me. "I can't have kids. I'm sterile. I found out a few years ago."

Wow, I wasn't expecting that. My heart goes out to him because even though I don't want children, I can't imagine how it would feel not to have a choice.

A dull headache begins behind my eyes, and I rub my forehead. "I'm sorry about that. I really am, but, did it ever occur to you to ask me what I want, because kids don't even come close to making the list. And I don't see the point in marriage."

That's truer than ever after the ring fiasco today.

"I know. I should've talked to you. I don't really know why I reacted that way."

He looks so miserable all I want to do is wrap my arms around him, but I also have my own heart to protect. "Noble, I get it. I've spent years taking care of my mom, worrying I'm not going to make rent, or be able to get her meds. I know what it's like to have anxiety knock you on your ass."

"So, you'll take me back?" I hate to douse the hope in his eyes, but I can't just jump back in.

"I just need a little time to think."

He nods, getting to his feet. "I understand." His gaze locks on mine. "I love you Jani. That's not going to change, no matter your decision."

I can't resist pulling him into my arms. "I love you too. Just give me a couple of days, okay? To get my own head together."

"Okay."

I step back and pull up his sleeve, revealing an equally pink arm. "Now, why do you look like a giant penis?"

His smile is shy and embarrassed. "Google *science experiment fail*. It's already all over Youtube, thanks to Kenny." He runs his fingers over my wrist. "You're still wearing my bracelet."

"It's pretty. It's not the bracelet's fault you were a dick."

He chuckles and shakes his head. "Can I call you in a couple of days?"

"Yeah."

I walk him to the door, and stare after him a little too long when he walks away. My sigh feels like it comes from my entire body. I hate this emotional shit. I understand Noble's anxiety better than I'd like to admit. Mine just happens to be more focused on relationships than anything else.

There's no doubt in my mind I love Noble. I'm just not sure loving anyone is such a great idea at the moment.

Chapter Eleven

Noble

"Hey, you're not black!" Trey exclaims as I walk through the front door. Apparently, they didn't get enough teasing in earlier when I came home to shower. I scrubbed for an hour, until all our hot water was gone, but all I managed to do was take my skin from red to pink.

The video I told Jani about is paused on the T.V. like they've just been waiting for me to get home so I can watch that clusterfuck again. I swear I'm going to kick Kenny's ass.

I'm saved from further torture by loud cursing coming from Denton's room. Trey, Kenny, and I all look at each other, then head down the hall. It takes a lot for Denton to lose his cool, so something is up.

His door is ajar, and he goes to push it shut, but Kenny catches it and swings it open. Denton stands there in his underwear, wide eyed, with a disgusted sneer on his face. "Crabs! That bitch gave me crabs!"

It takes a second for me to realize he's talking about Chloe with the silent C and L. Trey glances at me, then we all break into laughter.

"Fuck off! It's not funny! I have to shave my junk now. I'll look like a damn kid!"

His rant just makes us laugh harder.

"Relax, dude," Kenny says, his words broken by a chuckle. "I've had them before. You get the shampoo from the pharmacy and trim. You don't have to go bald. I'll loan you my mirror."

Denton's brow crinkles. "What the hell do I need a mirror for?"

"You lay it on the floor and squat over it. How else are you going to see what you're doing?"

Trey's face is red, and he looks like he's going to have a stroke or piss himself, one or the other. He stumbles out of the room to catch his breath, laughter still rocking his body.

"Oh god," Denton moans. He gives me a desperate look. "You have to go to the pharmacy with me."

"Dude, I'm pink."

"I'll tell you how to get the food coloring off."

That son of a bitch. "You know a way, and you didn't tell me?"

His lip twitches, but he doesn't manage an actual smile. "I was going to...eventually. Come on. You'd have done the same thing."

Yeah, I would have.

"Fine, tell me and I'll go with you."

He jerks on a pair of jeans and a shirt. "White vinegar. It'll wash right off. I spilled a container of egg dye on me one Easter when I was a kid. That's what my mom used to get it off."

"All right. Let's go, but we're taking your car. No crustaceans allowed in mine."

"Tinkle face."

"Crabby patty."

The things you do for your friends. Ten minutes later, we're standing in the drug store while Denton studies the crotch pesticides. His gaze darts around, making sure there's no one near us that could see as he scoops up two boxes. Kenny insisted he get a spray for the furniture and stuff, even though it's rare to pass them to someone else in that way.

I'm supposed to be the lookout. You'd think he'd learn, especially since he let me go to Jani and pour my heart out looking like a giant hemorrhoid. The girl he's been talking to from the gym, the one he met after his spectacular fall off the treadmill, rounds the corner, a bottle of aspirin in her hand.

Denton forgets why he's here and more importantly, what's in his hand when she smiles at him. "Hi, Denton. I thought that was you."

"Darcy, hey."

Her gaze settles on the products in his hand, and she instinctively takes a step back.

The horror blooming on Denton's face is almost too severe to be funny.

Almost.

"I've got to run, but I'll pick you up Saturday. Eight o'clock, right?"

A shudder runs through her. Literally. I've never seen a person shudder like that before. "I-um, I have a…thing. I might have to go to. I'll…call you, okay?"

The last words leave her mouth as she flees the scene like the little guys might jump out of his pant leg and mount an attack.

Denton's face is redder than mine, and he lays his face in his palm. "She's not going to call."

"Odds are against it."

I grab two big bottles of white vinegar on our way to the register. "Do you ever feel like someone made a huge mistake expecting us to be adults?"

"Every day," he sighs. "I used to think I'd hit an age where I suddenly felt like an adult. Like I'd know how to solve any problem, the way it seemed like my parents could. Fuck, everyone is just winging it, aren't they? Just stumbling along, trying not to screw up."

"I think we just discovered the secret of life."

The ride home is silent, and we part ways, him to take care of his crotch crickets, and me to douse myself in vinegar.

It smells terrible, but at least I'm not pink anymore.

Lying in bed an hour later, my phone beeps and my pulse races when I see it's Jani.

Jani: I returned the ring. The one we found in the river.

Wow. She actually tracked the woman down. I know she was eager to hear the story behind it.

Me: I'll bet she was happy to have it back. Was it the love story you thought it would be?
Jani: Her ex-husband chucked it in the river because she cheated with the neighbor, then divorced him after twenty years. He was glad to get it back, but only because she sued him for it.
Me: That sucks. I'm sorry it was so disappointing.
Jani: Yeah. I just thought you'd like to know. Good night.
Me: Good night.

I want to type so much more. I love you. Please put me out of my misery and take me back. But I promised to give her a couple of days of space, and I want to respect it.

I toss the phone on my night stand, and try to sleep. I've never wanted to put a day behind me so badly.

The next morning finds us all sitting around the living room, brooding for different reasons. Denton has no chance with his crush, and Kenny is struggling with his grades while his parents ride his ass. Trey is the only one in a decent mood. I swear that guy just glides through life with a smile no matter what happens.

"You need a grand gesture," Denton announces out of the blue, pointing at me.

"What?"

"To win Jani back. You need a grand gesture. You know, like those chick flicks. The guy screws up and does some sappy, over the top thing to show the girl he loves her."

"That's not a bad idea," Kenny says. "I don't have a boombox to hold over your head. Not sure a phone bluetoothed to a little speaker would have the same clout."

A grand gesture. An idea pops into my head, but it's crazy. Surely, they'd never let me, but after yesterday's fiasco, I don't have a lot to lose. Jumping to my feet, I grab my coat and head down to WFUK.

If this works, I'll have forfeited my man card for good, and I'll never live it down.

For Jani, I'll take the chance.

Harrison laughs his booming laugh as I stand, fidgeting, in his office. "You've got balls, boy, I'll give you that. After yesterday, I thought you might not come back at all. Are you sure you want to do that?"

Shrugging, I can feel the heat in my face. "It's for a girl."

Leaning back in his seat, he nods. "Yeah, they make us do crazy things. Just last year I took my wife square dancing for our anniversary. Do I look like the type of guy who square dances?"

A snort of laughter leaps out of me. He doesn't look like the type of guy who leaves his chair unless food is involved. "No, sir, you don't."

"It's worth it, though, to keep them happy. I'll tell you what. You come in at nine tomorrow, right? Be ready after your shift for the five fifteen slot. Who am I to stand in the way of love?" He chuckles. "This ought to be something."

"Thank you."

Now, I need Cassidy's help.

She returns my text and invites me to her house. I'm glad Wyatt isn't home to listen in as we talk.

"So, two questions. Do you think she'll like it? And can you make sure she sees it?"

Cass beams at me. "I'll say this for you, when you make a mistake, you go all out to fix it. I'm sure she'll be flattered, and yes, I'll make sure she doesn't miss it."

Cass isn't the only help I need, so I rush back to Violent Circle.

As soon as I park in front of the apartment, I know something is up. Laughter spills out the front door as I open it, and I gaze around at the crowd that has gathered here since I left. It looks like every neighbor under forty is here, and a few of the old timers as well.

Denton stands at the head of the dining room table, a piece

of paper spread out before him. "Okay, so we have the naked aspect covered. Who has sex toys handy?"

A few hands go up, along with some snorts and laughter. What the fuck is going on?

"Of course, Samantha has her hand up," Kenny jokes, and Samantha flips him off. It's all in good fun, though to be honest, the girl has been on more wieners than ketchup.

"Denton! What the hell, dude?"

Denton grins and passes me the paper. "Remember when I said that the new apartment management now wants to do monthly inspections? Along with imposing a bunch more bullshit rules? Well, the first inspection is in a few days. If they want to invade our privacy every month, we're going to give them something to see."

I scan over the list and it really is ridiculous. Monthly "housekeeping" inspections where they come in and judge how well you're keeping the apartment clean. A ton of new rules that are completely asinine. No sidewalk chalk. Apparently, it's considered graffiti. No wading pools or sandboxes for the kids. No barbecue grills, bicycles, or other outdoor items can be left outside when not in use. It gets even more ridiculous when you get to the consequences.

No toys can be left in the yard or on the stone porches. Everything has to be stored inside. Because that's easy when you already have no extra rooms or closet space. If they find a bicycle, tricycle, or toddler ride-on toy left out unsupervised in the yards, they'll take them to the office and it'll cost five dollars to get them back.

They can't be serious. Owning a property doesn't give a landlord the right to steal your child's toys, then hold them for ransom. It's illegal as hell. It has to be. Then there's the community service clause, or what Denton is referring to as the slavery amendment. All adults who don't have a full-time job, or aren't a full time student, have to volunteer ten hours per week.

Now, if we were talking about a lazy guy living here who refuses to work so he can benefit from nearly free rent, I'd understand this. The requirement may not sound too bad until you realize "volunteer" means to work for housing management, cutting grass, cleaning out apartments, and stuff like that, not spending time at a nursing home or animal shelter.

It would also apply to the families where one spouse works and the other stays home with the kids. Even if they're paying the top tier rent, as much as you'd pay at any apartment complex, the stay at home parent would have to find a babysitter or leave their kids to work for free, just to stay here.

A lot of this may not affect me or my friends, but it will hurt our neighbors.

"I'm in. What are we doing?"

"How do you feel about watching gay porn on the living room T.V.?" Denton asks.

"If you'll let me borrow some, sure."

Hoots of laughter fill the room, and I dodge Denton's fist.

"Hey! I never agreed to fisting!"

Denton flips me off, then returns to making plans with half our neighborhood. If there's one thing Violent Circle does well, it's pull together when things gets bad. We may be going about this in a funny way, but the situation isn't amusing. The consequences for failing a housekeeping inspection more than once is eviction, and some of us don't have anywhere else to go. It costs a lot to come up with a deposit, and first and last month's rent on a new place, not to mention so many here have lousy credit, or none at all due to our age. And that volunteer shit? No way.

The pretty new redhead who moved into Cassidy's old place sits on the edge of the sofa, with Neal not far away. The way he looks at her when she laughs displays the fact that Denton doesn't have a chance with this one, even if she has found out he isn't really gay.

"Neal, just the guy I need to talk to. Is Bailey here?"

Bailey is Neal's ten-year-old daughter. Yeah, I'm about to pull a kid into my win back Jani attempt.

"No, she's watching Veronica's little boy. Why? What's up?"

I explain my plan to him, and he slaps me on the back. "I'm

sure she'd love to do it. I'll have her there about five. Does that work?"

"Absolutely. Tell her there's a twenty dollar bill in it for her. Just call me if she doesn't want to, so I can find someone else."

The get together breaks up, with everyone understanding their part in sticking it to the new management, and I lock myself in my room, listening to music, and practicing for tomorrow, when I'm going to make a grade-A fool of myself for the woman I love.

I mean, I already modeled bondage gear for her. What's one more embarrassing moment in my life?

When I open my eyes the next morning, I'm shocked by how well I slept. Maybe because I haven't slept for shit since Jani and I broke up, or maybe because I feel better now that I have a plan.

The work day drags by, and I'm greeted with far too many snickers and grins, though whether it's from my last stunning display of incompetency or my upcoming humiliation, I'm not sure.

Finally, the clock shows me it's time, and I look up into Bailey's smiling, excited face. "Noble! I can't believe I get to do this! I told all my friends at school, but they didn't believe me. So Dad is recording it! Thank you!"

"Thanks for helping me. I know how good you are, so you are the first one I thought of. Do you have it down?"

"Oh yeah, I know it by heart."

Taking a deep breath, I wipe the sweat from my neck. "Okay, kid. Let's do this."

Chapter Twelve

January

"I'm on my way! For the love of dick, woman, what is so damned important?"

Cassidy invited me to dinner tonight with her and Wyatt, and wouldn't take no for an answer. Not that I would've refused, but when I suggested stopping off on the way to her house for a cake or something to bring for dessert, she damn near bit my head off.

"I'm pulling in your driveway now. It's just past five o'clock. Since when do you guys eat like senior citizens?"

"Bite me. I'm eating for two."

I end the call and park my car. She's waiting at the door like an excited puppy. Something is going on here. Maybe she has news she didn't want to tell me over the phone. She's already married and pregnant, what more could happen to her?

"Oh shit. Are you having twins?" I ask, stepping inside.

An indignant look crosses her face, and she looks down at her flat belly. "What? No!"

"You aren't showing, you psycho. You just look like you have big news."

Grabbing my arm, she pulls me into the living room. "I don't have news, but you need to see the news. Trust me."

She flops down on the couch in front of the television,

pulling me down beside her. Wyatt waves from his recliner. Maybe he can clue me in on why my best friend is acting crazy.

"Is this like a hormone thing or something? Postpartum psychosis, maybe?"

He laughs, and Cass smacks my arm. "Postpartum means after the birth, genius. Just watch."

They return from a commercial and the newscaster smiles into the camera. "We have a special segment today to welcome a new member of the WFUK family. You may have seen him a few days ago when he filled in for The Science Dude, and we're happy to say he decided to stay after we threw him unprepared into the deep end. Since he was such a good sport, we'd like to introduce him to our audience. Noble, come on out."

My head jerks back at the sound of his name, and a rush of adrenaline tingles through my body. I can't believe what I'm seeing.

Noble steps into sight, his hand on a little girl's shoulder. That's Bailey! Neal's daughter. She's clutching a guitar with an excited smile on her face.

"Hi, I'm Noble Bradley and this is Bailey Chambers." He smiles down at her. "She's an amazing guitar player and she's going to help me try to win back my girl today."

Oh god. He wouldn't.

"See, I screwed up a really good thing with the most beautiful woman in the world. She's funny, and caring, and smart. I'm completely and totally in love with her. What better way to show her than humiliating myself on television, right?"

Wyatt snorts out a laugh, but it barely registers.

"January Dixon, I love you, and if you take me back, I promise not to screw up again." He pauses. "No, that's probably impossible. Okay, I promise to do my best to make you happy and keep the screw ups as few and far between as possible."

My eyes well up as I giggle at his honesty.

"And since I can't express myself quite as good as him, I'm going to sing a song from Ed Sheeran, who can say the right words better than I can."

Oh no. This is extremely sweet and over the top romantic,

but here's the issue. I've heard Noble sing. God knows I love him, but the man couldn't carry a tune if it was stapled to him. This is going to be horrible.

Bailey strums her guitar and her notes ring out strong and clear. The girl is good. She's all smiles until Noble belts out the first line. Though her mouth falls open like a fish gasping for oxygen, her playing doesn't show her shock.

His face is beet red, but he faces the camera and sings—or tries to—the lyrics to Perfect, my favorite song by Ed Sheeran. I pretty much wore it out while we were together, so I'm not surprised he knows the words.

But, oh god, what he's doing to them. Ed would be horrified.

Wyatt nearly falls out his chair laughing, and Cass turns to me, her eyes wide with horror. "Oh, that's so bad, Jani," she whispers.

"Hey, it's the thought that counts."

"Does that mean you'll give him another chance?"

Watching the most adorable man on the planet squeak and croak his way through my favorite love song, I nod. "I had already decided to get back together. I just needed a little time, you know."

Wyatt laughs harder. "So he did this for nothing? Classic."

I toss a throw pillow at him. "It's not for nothing!"

Cass does the same, only her pillow smacks him in the head. "It's romantic! She'll never forget this!"

"That's for sure," I mumble. "Seriously, though, it's the sweetest thing anyone has ever done for me. If you give him shit over it, I'll tell everyone you let Cass fuck you with a strap on."

His mouth falls open. "I do not! Nothing has ever breached that area!"

"You own a sex toy shop. Who do you think people are going to believe?"

I smile sweetly at him while he grumbles. "Fine."

Noble finishes the song and smiles at the camera before it jumps back to the anchors, who share a look of amused horror. I don't hear what they say next because I'm on my feet, zipping my jacket.

"I've got to go the station."

"I'll drive you," Cass exclaims, slipping on her shoes.

Wyatt follows behind us, holding up his palms when I turn to glare at him. "I won't say a word. But I'm not missing this."

I'm in too much of a hurry to argue.

My mind is moving almost as fast as my speeding heart on the drive to WFUK. The man at the door smiles and allows us inside as soon as I tell him my name. I'm not sure how I'll react when I see Noble. I'm suddenly overwhelmed by too many emotions.

When his blond head appears around a corner, I tackle him. Literally. I jump into his arms and cover his mouth with mine, ignoring the hoots and cheers filling the hall around us.

Our lips smack loudly as we part, and I stare down into blue eyes brimming with joy. "You crazy asshole. I love you too. I can't believe you did that."

He kisses me again, his arms wrapped around me tight. "Does that mean we're back together?"

"Yes, but I need you to understand something. Next time you have a problem or things aren't going well, you talk to me. You don't ignore me for days. I don't deserve that shit and I'm not taking it from anybody."

"Understood. I'm sorry. I didn't mean to hurt you."

"I forgive you. No more sorries. I'm sure I'll screw things up too." I loosen the vice grip my legs have on his hips, and he sets me down, his fingers sweeping a lock of hair from my face. "I missed you."

"Me too, sweetheart."

"Are you off the clock? Can we get out of here? Because I really need a date with the porn penis."

He steps back, his posture stiffening, muscles standing out in his neck. "Where did you hear that?"

Aw. He's so cute looking all shocked. "A table full of girls at the coffee shop. I'm afraid I may have endangered your future career as a porn star by setting them straight. They were very disappointed."

His gaze is as cautious as his question. "It doesn't bother

you?"

"Noble, we all have a past. I'm not exactly innocent, you know."

"I'm aware." Leaning down, he brushes his lips over my ear. "Innocent girls don't give head as good as you do."

"I'm flattered. Let's go test that theory."

His arm falls around my shoulders as we walk out to the cars. "Hey Cass, thanks for everything," he shouts.

"Anytime." She grins at us, then shakes her head at Wyatt who looks like he's bursting to say something.

"Pegging, Wyatt. If you don't know that word, look it up," I warn in a singsong voice.

His lips press together, and he gets in the car without a word. Noble frowns down at me. "Did you just threaten to fuck him?"

Cassidy's gaze locks with mine, and we both break into laughter.

"And, everyone is in on this?" I ask, as Noble fills me in on the plan to make the management wish they'd never thought of inspections. We've worn ourselves—and my vagina—out over the last twenty-four hours, so we're just lounging on the couch together.

"Yeah, although half of them aren't doing anything. We don't want it to look like we're trying to stop them from coming in each month. It has to look like this is business as usual on the circle. They need to think this is what they'll be going through every time they come to snoop."

"What should I do?"

Noble glances around my half empty apartment. "Your place is so clean. Maybe we should go for a too clean scenario."

"Since all Mom's stuff is gone, I took the opportunity for a little spring cleaning."

His face softens, and he strokes my leg. "How are you doing with that?"

"I miss her, but I'm adapting. I think I may like living alone. What do you mean by too clean?"

He kisses my head and wraps his arms tighter around me. "Well, since eviction is what they're threatening, naturally people would be paranoid their apartments aren't clean enough. So, we douse your bathroom and kitchen with bleach, mop the floors with vinegar, make it so you can't breathe in here. They've made it clear you don't have to be home for the inspection, so you wouldn't have to stay and suffer with it. Afterward, we'd just have to open windows for a bit, rinse the surfaces and floors."

"Devious. I love it. What are you and the guys doing?"

"I'll be watching gay porn."

Giggles spill out of me. "Make sure you're in bed with your hands under the covers. They'll assume the worst."

"Oh, I'll be in the living room. The other guys will all be at work or school. But a throw blanket is a great idea."

"This is going to be amazing." I cuddle into him.

His fingers entwine in my hair, gently tugging the strands. "You haven't heard the best part. They've decided to put a tenant on the housing board. It's all for show of course, it's not like we'd get a vote in anything, but that tenant will be present at inspections."

"Who is the chosen tenant?"

"Neal, and he volunteered to wear a camera to record the whole thing. Everyone is meeting that night to see the video. Trey has a projector, so we're going to project it on the wall of the laundry room once it gets dark."

"I can't wait." I lean my head back against his shoulder, reveling in the scent of him. "Do you really think it'll change anything, though?"

"I don't know, but we have to start somewhere. A few of their rules have to be illegal. Neal has a friend who's a lawyer. He sent the paper to him to check out what can be fought."

"Well, the first inspection is tomorrow, so I'd better go get some bleach and vinegar."

I stand up to stretch and hear a tentative tap on the front door. The new girl, Veronica, stands on the porch, holding a bag and wearing a sheepish smile. "Hi, I know we haven't met. I'm Veronica. I just moved into two-oh-seven."

"Come in. I'm Jani."

She enters, and Noble waves from the couch. "Oh, hi, Noble. I'm just going around trying to collect some candles for the inspection."

Noble chuckles and explains. "She's going to burn scented candles, potpourri, fill the place with air freshener."

"So, the opposite of my bleach and vinegar disaster," I point out, and Veronica laughs.

"Ooh, that's a good one."

I have a few scented candles and a can of some flowery air freshener that I hand over. "I also have a can of Ozium, but that stuff smells like hospital disinfectant, so I think it'll work better here."

"Thanks, it was nice meeting you. I'll see you at the laundry room tomorrow night."

After she leaves, I flop back onto the couch. "Are your friends stalking that poor girl yet?"

"Nope, I think Neal has made it clear he's interested. They're both single parents, so they have that in common. Okay." He slaps my ass. "Let's get this place super clean."

It's funny as we prepare for this first inspection, I see all the neighbors out doing the same. I'm sure the maintenance men who witness it just think everyone is nervous and cleaning, the way they'd like us to be.

I almost feel sorry for the management. I mean, they're new here, so they have no idea what Violent Circle is capable of when we all join together.

A smile creeps across my face.

Chapter Thirteen

Noble

The guys have our apartment all cleaned up, and there's nothing going on that would break any of their rules, so I know they won't be able to say anything about what they see. After all, we live here, and everything we've arranged for the neighbors to do is perfectly within a tenant's rights to do in their own home. That includes watching porn in the living room.

Being buck naked in your own home is also acceptable, and boy, are they going to get an eyeful of some of my friends today. I'm glad the inspections start after the school bus picks up all the children for school.

After the last two nights I've spent with Jani, nothing can wipe the smile off my face. I don't know why I panicked the way I did. I'm so much happier with her. She doesn't add stress to my life, it's just the opposite. I don't worry about much of anything when she's near, and I know she's always got my back.

She stayed with me after we cleaned up her place, and we went back this morning before she went to work to toss some more bleach and vinegar around, topping it off by spraying almost a whole can of the ultra-concentrated hospital grade disinfectant. Whew. We were both choking and had to beat a quick retreat outside.

I toss a throw blanket on the couch and grab Kenny's tablet. It doesn't take me long to find a porn site featuring some hardcore guy on guy action, and cast it to the living room television. I'm so glad Denton opted for the fifty inch screen when he got his tax return last year. I make sure the surround sound is working and turn the volume up loud enough that you can just carry on a conversation over it. Not excessive, but annoying, more so because of the sounds emanating from it. Ugh, it sounds like a bulldog eating oatmeal. I don't want to look.

Shit. I looked. And props to that guy who obviously has a much higher pain tolerance than me. I had a girl stick her thumb in my ass once, unexpectedly. It hurt in a unique way I never plan to feel again.

My phone lights up with a text from Barney, letting me know the inspections have begun. We have him as a lookout, but he isn't going to do anything to antagonize them. He'll be lucky to pass the inspections as it is, although I know a couple of neighbors helped him get his place cleaned up.

There's nothing to do now but wait. The minutes tick by as the video goes from one couple to another. These two guys must be the romantic type since they're making out on a beach. That is not a place I'd want to get sand in.

My phone beeps with a message from Jani.

Jani: The suspense is killing me.
Me: They're on the way now. Should be here any minute.
Jani: Enjoying the movie?
Me: Way too much hairy ass in it for me.
Jani: The guys usually wax.
Me: How would you know?
Jani: Got to get back to work.
Me: Busted. Dirty girl.

I've shut and locked the front door, and though my car is out front, they barely tap on the door before coming in.

Neal is first, and I see him stifle a smile as he stands to the side, trying to make sure the camera in his glasses catches everything that's going on. He's followed inside by a man, a woman in her mid-thirties, and a woman who must be over sixty.

Their expressions are priceless.

I'm sprawled on the couch, one hand thrown across my bare chest, the other tucked beneath the blanket. I have shorts on, but they can't tell. "What the hell?" I exclaim, sitting up. The onscreen couple are in the middle of a vigorous blow job, and the audio coming through the speakers sounds like someone is stirring a cooked pot of macaroni.

"The first inspection is today, Mr." The gruff sounding man pauses until I reply.

"Bradley."

"Mr. Bradley. We're here to check on things."

"Oh, right, I think I heard about that." I fall back and wave them on. "Have a look around then."

The older woman's mouth falls open. I guess she expected me to turn off the video, maybe run away in embarrassment. The younger woman gives me a sideways look, and I swear her lips twitch like she's restraining a laugh.

They make a quick trip through the apartment, but with the surround sound on and the volume at this level, there's no escaping the man party going on in the living room.

The onscreen characters choose that moment to get vocal.

"Oh, yes, lick that cock."

"You want it in your ass, don't you? Tell me you want my cock in your ass."

When they return to the living room, the man shoves a paper and clipboard at me. "Sign here. Just says we inspected and everything was fine."

"Sure, just give me a sec to read it. I never sign anything without reading it."

It's a short form, but I take my time, making them stand there while the guys on the T.V. graduate to rimming. The older lady lets out a squeak, then rushes out the front door. Finally, I sign the paper, and they leave. Neal grins at me before he steps out the door.

Nailed it.

No pun intended.

"It's time!" Jani squeals, grabbing her coat. The weather has cooperated with us tonight, warming up far more than normal for this time of the year, as if it too supports our cause. I returned to Jani's apartment and opened her windows while she was at work, so it's mostly aired out. It was a good hour after they left that I showed up, but it still made my eyes water just walking through the door, so I can imagine how it was when they came in. We've spent the last hour rinsing the over bleached and vinegar drenched areas.

I'm as excited to see the video as Jani is after some of the stories I've heard today. Everyone did their part and then some. Pulling my coat on, I grab a fold up camping chair while Jani grabs another, and we head down the road. It's full dark, and everyone is gathered on the lawn facing the laundry room wall, laughing and exchanging stories.

There are no kids present, obviously, and with it being so far after business hours, no way anyone from housing management is going to see this.

Too bad.

Neal and Denton walk out and wave their hands, getting our attention so it'll quiet down. "Okay," Neal says. "I managed to get footage in every apartment, and Denton has edited it down to the ones that participated. Everyone did fantastic, but I think I have to throw a couple special mentions out there to Noble and his jacking off to gay porn show, and Mallory and Dennis for actually making one of them vomit."

"Hey, they saw me blowing a guy!" Samantha calls, sounding defensive.

"Like that's out of the ordinary," I murmur, and Jani elbows me, giggling.

Neal nods to Denton before he walks off to join Veronica.

"Okay, let's see it. I believe Veronica's place is first. She went a little overboard with scented candles and air freshener."

The wall jumps to life with an image of Veronica's living room as the three inspectors come in behind Neal. Instantly, their hands go to their mouths. "I-I'm allergic to flowers," the older lady stutters and retreats back outside.

Onscreen Veronica smiles brightly. "There are no real flowers. I just wanted to freshen the place up for the inspection. Please, come in."

Yeah, this girl is going to fit right in here.

We watch, as the three inspectors are assaulted, apartment after apartment, without ever being touched. One apartment is filled with the scent of cooking cabbage and chitlins that have been boiling overnight. Another features two tenants faking the flu, cuddled up in blankets on the couch, retching and dumping fake vomit into basins. You can't blame someone for being sick.

All of the inspectors are green after leaving there, and there's a time gap before they move onto the next as they try to gather themselves. The next apartment is Samantha's, and everything looks normal until they open her bedroom door to find her gobbling a knob wearing only a pair of panties.

Looking up at them, she feigns surprise, then outrage. "Hey, this show aint free!" The man she's with just shrugs at them, looking bored.

They don't have much luck at the next apartment either, where sex toys are scattered across the living room. Leaving the dishwasher open where an array of dildos and butt plugs drip dry was a pretty good touch.

You'd think they'd learn, but no. They go to the bedroom where a massive St. Andrews Cross stands, displaying a selection of handcuffs and spanking implements. "We can thank Jani for that set up!" Stephanie calls out. "I'll return it to Scarlet Toys tomorrow."

"Now, let's not get too hasty," her husband interjects, making everyone laugh.

One of the tenants even brought their three-year-old twins

into the fun by having them "play a game" where they scratch their heads. She was very apologetic about the head lice, but they caught it at pre-school, so she could hardly be blamed.

Finally, they get to Mallory and Dennis's place. The three inspectors who were so eager just an hour ago now look bedraggled and weary. Mallory invites them in with a smile, but what you don't see is Dennis, dropping the mother of all stink bombs in the bathroom.

Mallory chats with them in the living room and just as they walk past the bathroom, Dennis bursts out, a magazine tucked under his arm. "Whew! You may want to give that a minute! I swear I shit stuff I ate when I was ten!"

"Dennis!" Mallory pretends to scold him.

"What? I ain't kiddin, woman! I saw corn! I ain't had corn in years!"

It's at that moment, the stench really hits, rolling out of the bathroom and down the hall. The lady in her thirties clamps a hand over her mouth and races for the front door. She manages to make it to the street before throwing up. Neal follows her, asking if she's okay, so we don't get to see the other's reactions after, but Mallory speaks up.

"They were right behind her. Didn't even look in the bedrooms!"

"I think we can call this a success!" Denton announces, and everyone cheers.

I grin down at Jani. "Do you think they learned anything?"

Jani wraps her arms around me. "Don't fuck with Violent Circle."

"That's right, baby."

Epilogue

January
3 years later

"I can't believe you're doing this," Cassidy says for at least the fourth time. "I'm going to kill Wyatt for opening a Scarlet Toys there."

"It's freezing cold all the time. Who needs sex toys more than people who spend so much time indoors? Besides, I can take classes while Noble works. It's not forever." I lean down to brush my hand over her daughter's hair.

"She's going to miss you, too."

Yeah, moving to Alaska isn't going to be easy. I'm leaving everyone I know and love, except Noble. I'm terrified and more excited than I've ever been in my life. It's an adventure, an opportunity I never thought I'd get. When Noble was offered a research position at the University of Alaska in Fairbanks, we were faced with a serious decision. He was tempted to pass it up and accept a lesser job somewhere else because of me, and I couldn't let him do that.

I've spent the last two years paying off all my debt and saving money. With just myself to take care of and the well-paying position at Scarlet Toys, I got ahead quickly. Noble and I had plans to move in together after his graduation, but the Alaska thing came out of the blue.

I had already decided to go with him, and take the business classes I've been saving for, when Wyatt announced he'd been considering a few small towns in Alaska, and Fairbanks would be a perfect location to open his next store.

So, here we are, all packed up, ready to catch a plane tomorrow. Violent Circle has come together to throw us both a going away party tonight. I have one more night with all my friends before I move over thirty-five hundred miles away.

"You'd better video chat with me every day," I warn Cass, before bending to talk to her two-year-old daughter. "You too, Kiera. Do you want to talk to aunt Jani on the computer?"

Her little face lights up with a smile. "Yes! I like the computer!"

I know she doesn't really understand, but I'm going to stay in touch as much as I can. She looks up at me. "Aunt Jani, Alaska has polar bears."

"I know they do."

"Don't get eat by a polar bear, 'kay?"

Cass smiles and holds back a giggle. "Nope, I'll stay far away from the polar bears."

Kiera thinks for a moment, her chubby finger tapping her chin. "Are there frickin elephants there?"

My gaze jumps to Cass, who stares down at her little clone. "Kiera, don't say frickin. It's not a nice word."

Kiera's little forehead rumples and she runs off toward her bedroom, returning with a picture book of animals. Jumping on my lap, she opens the book and points to a page. "See, it's a frickin elephant, Mommy. That's not a bad word."

Cass and I follow her finger to the picture in question, and I can't stop the giggles from pouring out of me. Kiera stares at us both as we try to stop laughing, her expression growing indignant. "What? It is! Daddy told me! It's a frickin elephant!"

Cass composes herself first, and hugs her daughter. "African elephant, hun." She sounds out the word, and Kiera echoes her.

"No, there aren't any elephants there," I assure her.

I'm going to miss this kid.

Cass needs to put Kiera down for her nap, so I head back to my now empty apartment. There's nothing there but an inflatable mattress, since all our stuff has been shipped to our new home. Since tonight is going to be a late one, partying with the whole neighborhood, I take the opportunity for a quick nap.

Noble wakes me, his hand brushing through my hair. "Hey, the party is starting. Are you going to sleep all night?"

Shit. I guess all the excitement of the last week caught up with me.

"Mmm, I'm awake. Did you get everything taken care of at WFUK?"

"Yep. They had a little going away thing. Got me a cake and everything."

"That's sweet."

Noble looks down at me and it strikes me how much he's changed. His eyes are the same bright blue, and the same blond hair hangs long over his forehead, but his jaw has become more defined. He's lost the last of that baby-faced look and somehow transformed into this rugged, perfect male specimen.

"I never get tired of seeing that look," he murmurs, kissing my neck.

"What look?"

"The one that says you're thinking about my cock."

I tilt my head, ignoring the obnoxious squeak of the mattress. "I'm sorry to burst your bubble, but I wasn't thinking of Lord Farquad at all."

His teeth nip my neck. "Are those little dick jokes ever going to get old?"

"You spent six years being known as Porn Penis. I don't want your ego to get too big."

"You'll be happy to have a nice big porn penis to keep you warm once we get to our igloo."

Giggling, I push him off of me. "We aren't moving to an igloo. Fairbanks is a modern city."

He gives me the same grin that grabbed my heart three years ago. "Next you'll tell me that we don't need the tennis racket snow shoes I ordered."

Giggling, I lean my forehead against his. "We're really doing this."

His breath is soft on my face. "We really are. Are you scared?"

"Terrified? You?"

"A little nervous, but with you by my side, I can do anything."

"Together, we can do anything," I correct.

"Oh, before I forget, keep an eye on Trey tonight. I bought a tube of capsaicin like the one he used on my toilet the first night you stayed with me, and I rubbed it into every pair of underwear he owns."

I get to my feet. "You're the best boyfriend ever. Let's go. We have one more night of crazy."

"I'm going to miss this place."

"Me too, but maybe our new neighborhood will have people who throw dildoes into the yard, or run around naked." I slip on my shoes, and grab my jacket.

"It won't be the same." He wraps his arm around me, and we head for the door.

Flipping off the light for the last time, I take one final look back.

"No, there's no place like Violent Circle."

THE END

Don't miss out on Neal and Veronica's story in the final book of the Violent Circle Trilogy.

Thanks for reading! If you'd like to check out more of my work, I have two books that are always free!

Acknowledgements

This book was so much fun to write, mainly because so many expressed interest in January and Noble's story. And by expressed interest, I mean they messaged me with *When the hell do we get the next one*? There's no better feeling than knowing readers love the characters as much as I do.

To my betas, Veronica Ashley, Amanda Munson, Theresa O'Reilly, Bridget McEvoy, Lissa Jay, and Melissa Teo. Thank you so much for pointing out the embarrassing plot holes, mistakes, and typos, and keeping me from getting too ridiculous. You make me look much smarter than I am. Veronica, no one dies in this book, so there's no need to pee on anything I own.

Melissa Teo is also the best damn P.A. I could ask for, and I'm so grateful for how hard she works to get my books seen. Every time she messages me with *I have an idea*, I'm excited and terrified to see what her brain has conjured up this time. It's always epic. If you don't know who she is, hang your head in shame and then go check out these groups:

Booksmacked

B.A.N.G.

The cover was created by Ally Hastings at Starcrossed Covers, who never fails to deliver no matter what weird stuff I ask for. Fuzzy pink handcuffs? Solo cup and ping pong ball? Sure, no problem. Thanks again, Ally.

The pretty formatting is done by Angela Shockley at That Formatting Lady. She's awesome, but don't everyone start using her because I need her free to work her magic. I'll share, but just know I'm not happy about it.

To the Shady Ladies in my book group, thanks for making the group such a fun, drama free place to hang out. Thanks for getting my sense of humor and not thinking I'm crazy. Or at least keeping it to yourself if you do.

Last, but certainly not least, thanks to all the book bloggers, page owners, and group owners who work tirelessly to help me and so many other authors get their stories out there. We couldn't do any of this without you.

Stalking Links

I love to connect with readers! Please stalk me at the following links:
Friend me at:
https://facebook.com/authorsmshade

Like my page:
https://facebook.com/smshadebooks

Follow on Twitter:
https://twitter.com/authorSMShade

Visit my blog:
http://www.smshade.blogspot.com

Sign up for my monthly newsletter:
http://bit.ly/1zNe5zu

Would you like to be a part of the S.M. Shade Book Club? As a member, you'll be entered in giveaways for gift cards, e-books, and Advanced Read Copies. Be a part of the private Facebook group and privy to excerpts and cover art of upcoming books before the public. You can request to join at: https://facebook.com/groups/694215440670693

More by S.M. Shade

The Striking Back Series

Book 1: Everly

The first time I met Mason Reed, we were standing naked in a bank, surrounded by guns.

That should have been a warning.

An MMA champion, trainer, and philanthropist, but not a man who gives up easily, Mason is trouble dipped in ink and covered in muscle.

Growing up in foster care, I'm well aware that relationships are temporary, and I do my best to avoid them. After a sheet clenching one night stand, I'm happy to move on, but Mason pursues me relentlessly. Sweet, caring, protective, and at times, a bossy control freak, this persistent man has climbed inside my heart, and I can't seem to shake him.

After saving me from a life threatening situation, he's also won something much harder to obtain. My trust. But does he deserve it? Is his true face the one he shows the world? Or is his charitable, loving manner only a thin veneer?

This book contains sexual situations and is intended for ages 18 and older.

Book 2: Mason

From the moment I saw her, I wanted her in my bed.

I should've stopped there.

Everly Hall burst into my complicated life and changed it forever. I'm a fighter, but I had no defense against this beautiful, stubborn woman.

Now, I stand to lose everything I have, everything I am. My secrets are dangerous, and put more lives at stake than my own. I intended to tell her in time, but my time is up.

Everything rests on Everly.

This is the conclusion of Mason and Everly's story.

Contains violence and sexual situations and is intended for adults 18 and older.

Book 3: Parker

Hit it and quit it.

One and done.

Hump and dump.

That has been my philosophy on relationships for the last seven years. Don't get me wrong, I'm not a bad guy. I'm always upfront and truthful with the women I date. I don't promise them anything but a good time.

I could've gone on happily sleeping my way through the major metropolitan area if it wasn't for her. The dark haired beauty who haunts my days and keeps me awake at night. Strong and sweet, she makes me reconsider everything I believe about love.

Too bad she's completely off limits.

I've never been good at following the rules.

Book 4: Alex – An M/M Romance

Ninety- two days. Thirteen weeks. That's how long it's been since I lost my love, my best friend. It's been everything I can do to drag myself out of bed and get back to work, but I know Cooper would want me to move on. I think he'd even be happy if he knew who I want to move on with. The target of my affection, though, may not be so thrilled about my choice.

He's straight. Or he thinks he is.

A womanizer of the worst kind with a face and body that keeps a steady stream of willing women at his door, he seems happy to work his way through the entire female population. But there's no mistaking the way he looks at me when he thinks I'm not paying attention.

One way or another, I'll show him what he really wants.

This is book four of The Striking Back Series, but can also be read as a standalone novel.

Intended for 18 years and older. Contains sexual content, including sex between two men.

The In Safe Hands Series

Landon, Book One

Zoe

I'm not interested. I'm not interested in his blue-green ocean colored eyes, his lean muscular body, or that crooked smile that can be so infuriating. I have more important things to worry about, like how to keep myself in college and my sixteen year old brother fed and sheltered. We all know life is hard, some of us just learn that lesson younger than others, but that doesn't mean I'll give up. I intend to succeed and make sure my brother has the opportunities he deserves, and no privileged jerk is going to distract me.

Landon

I don't date. Don't get me wrong, I'm far from celibate, but my condition makes carrying on any kind of normal relationship impossible. My life revolves around In Safe Hands or ISH, the underground hacker group I work with to track down and take care of predators and sex offenders who beat the system. I'm satisfied with my life until the day I meet the smart mouthed, compassionate, determined woman who opens my eyes to possibilities I never thought existed.

Dare, Book Two

Ayda

I hear him.

His deep voice and rumbling laugh. The bang of the headboard slamming the wall and fake screams from yet another woman. Derek is a pile of muscle and ink, a bad boy fantasy only a few layers of wood and plaster away. It's all I expect or want him to be.

Until that irresistible voice begins talking to me.

Dare

I hear her.

The clicking of her fingers on a keyboard, her music or TV playing in the background. Her musical laugh and soft cries of pleasure, accompanied by a low, steady buzz. Ayda is a good girl who keeps to herself, and I have no business pursuing her, but I'm not a man known for doing the right thing.

I'm an ex-con. I'm a criminal.

And I want her.

Justus, Book Three

Justus

I'm not conceited.

Really, I'm not. It just so happens I have a body a Greek God would be jealous of, and a face that could make an angel weep. Other than that, I'm just your everyday normal guy who happens to take his clothes off for money. Sure, I've had to dispose of a few guys for In Safe Hands, the organization I work for that helps track predators and child molesters, but other than that, completely normal.

Women flock to me, screaming and paying for the right to touch me, so why is this woman so stubborn? Sadie Belmont's curvy body and sharp tongue have haunted me since I met her a year ago. There's something about her that gets stuck in my head like a bad song, and I'm determined to find out why I want her so badly, and why she can't stomach the thought.

Sadie

I can't believe I'm doing this. Of all the men in the world, I'm taking Justus Alexander to my childhood home in Oklahoma to meet my mother. A stripper who has a revolving door of women jumping in and out of his bed. Nine months ago when I lied to my mother and told her I had a steady boyfriend, I didn't expect it to come to this. She doesn't have long to live, and her only wish is to know I have a husband before she goes.

I can't disappoint her, and male escorts cost way more than I can afford, so when Justus volunteered, I took him up on his offer. I know what he wants. After annoying me with constant pick up lines for a year, he sees an opportunity to get me in bed. It's not going to happen. I just need to get through this week with my sanity intact.

Tucker, Book Four

Tucker

She's beautiful.

She's young.

She's driving me out of my mind.

I've always done my best to avoid Leah Bolt. I have enough problems without having to deal with a young woman with a crush. My life has been a disaster since I was court-martialed and dishonorably discharged from the military. After spending a year living on the streets, I'm finally starting to pull things together.

Now, I'm stuck with her, living side by side in my house with my complete opposite. If spending every day with this peppy, optimistic, energetic woman doesn't kill me, her brother will. Dare is a friend and a member of In Safe Hands, a group that tracks down sexual predators and brings them to justice. He has also done time and is the size of a mountain.

I've survived combat, but I may be taken down by a perky blond.

Leah

He's gorgeous.

He's older.

He's a stubborn, broody jerk.

Tucker Long is every woman's dream...until you talk to him. He may be sexy when he's out sweating in the sun with sawdust clinging to him as he hammers and saws, but try to hold a conversation and all you get are grunts and nods.

He was the one who wanted a house sitter and just because his plans fell through doesn't mean I'm changing mine. My future is up in the air while I try to decide who I want to be, and Tucker's farm is the perfect place for me to do it. He calls me kid, but the way he looks at me doesn't lie.

I may be ten years younger, but I can still handle him.

All that Remains – An MMF Menage Trilogy

The Last Woman, All That Remains: Book One

When Abby Bailey meets former model and actor, Airen Holder, in a darkened department store, romance is the last thing on her mind. A plague has decimated the population, leaving Abby to raise her son alone in a world without electricity, clean water, or medical care. Her only priority is survival.

Traumatized by the horror of the past months, Abby and Airen become a source of comfort for one another. Damaged by her past and convinced Airen is out of her league, Abby is determined to keep their relationship platonic. However, Airen is a hard man to resist, especially after he risks his life to save hers.

When a man named Joseph falls unconscious in their yard, and Abby nurses him back to health, everything changes. How does love differ in this new post-apocalyptic world? Can three unlikely survivors live long enough to find their place in it?

This is the first of the All that Remains series and can also be read as a stand alone novel. It contains violence and sexual situations and is recommended for ages 18 and older.

Falling Together, All That Remains: Book Two

In the aftermath of a global nightmare, Abby Holder is living her dream. Married to the love of her life, Airen, and surrounded by friends and family, it seems she's found her happily ever after.

But the struggle of living in a post-plague world is never ending. When circumstances take Airen far away, she's faced with the devastating realization he may be lost to her forever. Broken-hearted, she turns to Joseph, her best friend and the only one who understands her pain. After all, he loves Airen too.

The sound of a car horn in the middle of the night changes everything, leaving Abby caught between the two most important men in her life. After surviving the worst the world could throw at them, Airen, Abby, and Joseph must face the most brutal human experience...true love. Can they overcome the betrayal, the hurt feelings, and jealousy to do what's right for the ones they love?

Their circumstances are far from ordinary. Perhaps the answer is extraordinary as well.

This book includes sexual scenes between two men and is intended for ages 18 and older

Infinite Ties, All That Remains: Book Three
The more you look to the future, the more the past pursues you.

Abby, Airen, and Joseph have fought and suffered to come together. All they want is to move forward and raise their family with the love they never had.

Unfortunately, the re-appearance of former friends and enemies complicates their lives, threatening to expose closely guarded secrets. With a vital rescue looming, their relationship isn't the only thing at risk. Can they let go of the past in order to hang on to a future with each other?